The Abandoned

©2023 by Molly Britton

Contents

Chapter 1

The dawn light had yet to fully touch the murky London streets as the carriage rolled to a halt. Maggie Barlow, a slip of a girl with curly black hair and blue eyes that shone defiantly bright against her freckle-dotted, fair skin, looked upon the imposing red-brick workhouse that lay before them.

Inside the carriage, a stifling silence prevailed, broken only by the occasional sniffle from young William, and the quiet whimper of Thomas, just six years old. They sat huddled close, three birds cast from their nest, their innocent faces shadowed by fear and uncertainty.

Lottie Barlow, their mother, stared out at the workhouse gates, her gloved fingers fidgeting restlessly with the locket at her neck. "You'll be cared for," she said, her words hollow in the still air.

Maggie bit her lip, her heart thundering in her chest. She gathered her younger brothers closer, protective. Her voice emerged in a whisper. "Mother, we could...we could come with you."

Lottie stiffened, her gaze still fixed on the workhouse, the evidence of her choice. Her lips pursed, her eyes void of the warmth they used to hold. "You know that can't be, Margaret."

The silence reigned again, deafening in its intensity, pressing heavily on Maggie's shoulders. She felt William's fingers tighten around hers, saw Thomas bury his face into her dress. They were frightened, their small world rapidly fracturing. Maggie, despite her own fears, knew she had to be the stronghold.

With a jolt, the carriage door swung open, revealing the workhouse matron. She was a stern figure, her grey eyes devoid of warmth, her mouth set in a tight line. "Time to go, children," she said, her voice gratingly cold.

Maggie nodded, pulling her brothers from the carriage with the determination only a protective older sister could muster. She turned back towards her mother, hoping for a last-minute reprieve, a change of heart, a tearful hug.

Their mother simply nodded, her face unreadable, eyes dry. She watched as her children, her own flesh and blood, were taken away. Once they were out of sight, the carriage door was closed, the horses stirred. Their mother was off, to a life of comfort and luxury that had no room for three fatherless children.

Maggie watched the carriage roll away, her heartache echoing in the empty street. She swallowed hard, forced her trembling hands to still, her tears to dry.

She turned to the workhouse, the symbol of their new life. Her brothers clung to her, their tiny bodies trembling. Maggie, the freckled girl with bright blue eyes and unwavering spirit, wrapped her arms around them. And with a deep breath, she stepped forward, their only shield against the world that had turned so cruel.

The interior of the workhouse was as grim as its exterior, an echo of faded glory with dim-lit hallways and the musky scent of age. Mrs Bell, the stern matron, led them inside, her feet tapping against the stone floor in a rhythm that made Thomas whimper.

At the entrance, a large, wooden table awaited them, a repository for personal effects. Mrs Bell indicated towards it with a pointed finger. "Leave your belongings here," she said, her voice echoing in the vast hall.

Each of them only had a small bag, a meagre collection of the remnants of their previous life. Maggie hesitated, her eyes skimming over her brothers. William clung to a worn teddy bear, its single remaining button-eye staring back at her with an emptiness that mirrored their own. Thomas held a small wooden horse their father had whittled years ago, his last connection to the parent they'd lost.

With a sigh, she opened her bag, laying out a few dresses, a pair of shoes, and a locket with a small portrait of their parents. Thomas followed suit, placing his wooden horse on the table with a trembling hand. But William clutched his teddy tighter, his bottom lip quivering.

Mrs Bell huffed, crossing her arms. "Drop the bear, boy," she commanded, her patience worn thin.

But the sight of William's tear-filled eyes, his small body shaking, sparked a fire in Maggie. "He needs it, ma'am," she reasoned. "It comforts him."

Mrs Bell snatched the teddy bear from William, who wailed at the loss of his precious companion. "No personal belongings are allowed. Those are the rules," she snapped, her voice echoing in the cold, stone hall.

Maggie soothed William, whispering words of comfort, as Mrs Bell tossed the teddy bear into a box labelled 'Discard'. The youngest Barlow cried into Maggie's skirts, and even Thomas' eyes welled up at the sight.

Mrs Bell cleared her throat, the sound echoing in the quiet hall. "Boys are in the attic dormitory, girls in the west wing," she declared, her eyes cold as she surveyed them. "You'll be split up."

The words hung in the air, heavy as lead. Maggie's heart clenched at the thought.

They had lost their father, their mother had abandoned them, and now even the small comfort of their shared presence would be taken away.

But she swallowed down her fear, forcing a brave smile onto her face. "It's okay, William, Thomas. I'll be close, and we'll see each other every day," she assured, hoping her words held more conviction than she felt.

As Mrs Bell led them to their separate quarters, Maggie took a final look at the discarded teddy bear, the wooden horse, the remnants of their past life. The heartache in her chest intensified, but she held her head high.

William's cries reverberated through the harsh stone corridors of the workhouse, a painful counterpoint to the dreary silence. The stern-faced matron, Mrs Bell, paused, her steel-grey eyes narrowing at the sound.

"Quiet, boy," she barked, her voice as harsh and biting as the chill in the air. When William's cries only intensified, she turned and gave him a sharp reprimand, the back of her hand connecting with his cheek. The contact wasn't hard, but enough to stun William into shocked silence.

Maggie's heart lurched at the sight, her fingers curling into fists. "You've no right—," she started, her voice brimming with indignation. But a warning look from Mrs Bell silenced her.

"Silence, girl. Or you'll share your brother's punishment."

Thomas, who had been so quiet until now, whimpered at the threat. Maggie placed a calming hand on his shoulder, the gentle touch belying her own unease.

Mrs Bell's gaze narrowed as she studied Maggie. There was something about this girl, this defiant child, that unsettled her. Perhaps it was the fire in her blue eyes or the protective stance she took for her brothers. It irked her, this strength, this hope in such a dreary place.

"We'll have none of your stubbornness here, girl. Your brothers are off to the attic dormitory now, and you to the west wing," she declared with a finality that echoed through the silent hallway.

The separation was immediate, two broad-shouldered overseers stepping in to guide Thomas and William away. As they were led down the long corridor, their pleas for Maggie grew louder, their small voices piercing the quiet of the workhouse.

"Maggie!" Thomas cried, his small form struggling against the overseer's grip.

"Maggie, don't leave us!" William echoed, his tear-streaked face turning back towards his sister one last time before disappearing from sight.

Maggie felt her heart shatter as their cries echoed in her ears. She watched helplessly as her brothers were taken away, their pleas lingering in the cold air. She could only stand, rooted in place, her own tears threatening to spill over.

Mrs Bell moved to lead Maggie away, her fingers digging into Maggie's arm with an unkind grip. The girl didn't resist, her gaze fixed on the empty hallway, her mind spinning with thoughts and fears for her brothers.

She made a silent vow then, a promise echoed in the cold stones of the workhouse. She would find a way to protect her brothers, to keep them safe in this cruel place. She didn't know how yet, but she would figure it out. She had to.

As she was led to the west wing, the echoing cries of her brothers still fresh in her ears, Maggie Barlow clenched her fists. Her bright blue eyes, the mirror of her resolve, glistened with unshed tears. But her spirit was undimmed.

The workhouse was a place of despair, but Maggie would not let it break them. She was all her brothers had now, and she would not fail them.

The girls' dormitory in the west wing was a large, dim-lit chamber filled with rows of narrow iron beds. As Mrs Bell led Maggie in, a hush fell over the room, dozens of pairs of curious eyes peering out from under worn, thin blankets.

Before Maggie could take it all in, a sudden movement caught her eye. A girl, perhaps a little older than herself, bumped into Mrs Bell as she hurried past.

"Watch where you're going, you clumsy fool!" Mrs Bell snapped, her voice echoing through the room. The girl mumbled a quick apology, but the matron wasn't appeased.

"I didn't mean to, Ma'am," the girl said, her voice wavering. "I was just—"

Mrs Bell cut her off, a slap resounding through the silent dormitory. The girl stumbled back, holding her reddening cheek. "Another word, and you'll spend the night in the closet," Mrs Bell threatened.

Maggie could only watch in stunned silence, the harsh reality of the workhouse striking her like a blow.

Without another word, Mrs Bell led Maggie to an empty bed, the metal frame cold under her touch. "This is your place," she said, indicating the bare mattress and threadbare sheets.

The bed was a far cry from the soft mattress she had known back home. It was thin and uncomfortable, the sheets worn and barely sufficient to ward off the biting chill of the room.

As Mrs Bell left the room, the cold seeped in, unimpeded by the thin blankets. The girls in the dormitory remained silent, their gazes wary, their bodies hunched under the threadbare covers.

Maggie felt a lump forming in her throat, her heart aching for the comfort of her old home, her mother's warmth, her father's reassuring voice, the laughter of her brothers.

But she swallowed back her tears, pulling the thin blanket tightly around her. She wouldn't allow herself the luxury of tears, not here, not now. She had a mission – to protect her brothers, to survive this place.

As the sounds of the night crept in, the soft sobbing of some girls, the distant clatter of the workhouse machinery, Maggie found herself alone in her thoughts. She imagined William and Thomas in the attic dormitory, as cold and lonely as she was.

Her resolve hardened further, her determination ignited by the harsh reality of their situation. This was their life now, a test of their resilience. Maggie Barlow would not let it break them. She had a promise to keep, after all.

She curled up on the thin mattress, the cold metal frame beneath her a stark reminder of her vow. It was going to be a long night, and an even longer journey. However, she was ready to face it, for her brothers, and for herself.

Maggie lay wide awake in the biting cold, her heart heavy with worry. The thin, threadbare blanket offered little warmth, the hard mattress beneath her an unkind reminder of her new life. Her thoughts were filled with William and Thomas, their tear-streaked faces and desperate pleas echoing in her mind.

She hoped they were faring better, that the boys' dormitory was less daunting than the girls'. But reality reminded her that their plight was likely the same, their fears and uncertainties mirroring her own.

She squeezed her eyes shut, trying to banish the image of William's teddy bear tossed aside, the vacant look in their mother's eyes as she abandoned them, the harsh rebuke of the matron, the cold and uncaring walls of the workhouse.

Yet within her despair, there was a flicker of hope. Tomorrow, she would see her brothers. The common cafeteria, where all the workhouse children had their meals, would be the rendezvous. She yearned for their shared company, the comfort of their shared presence in this bleak new world.

Chapter 2

Three months later

Three months had passed since Maggie and her brothers had entered the bleak world of the workhouse. The days had been gruelling, an endless cycle of toil and drudgery that had worn away at their youthful spirits. Yet, they'd clung to the hope of each stolen moment together, each shared glance across the cafeteria, each whispered word of comfort.

On a sweltering mid-summer day, Maggie was knee-deep in the workhouse laundry, her hands red and raw from scrubbing. The hot sun beat down mercilessly, its blistering rays making the cold stones of the workhouse seem like a cruel mirage.

It was in this broiling heat that she saw her. An older girl, one of Mrs Bell's errand runners, approached, her pace quick and her face serious. "Maggie Barlow," she called, her voice cutting through the clamour of the laundry yard. "Mrs Bell wants to see you. And your brothers."

A flutter of anxiety coursed through her, her thoughts instantly darting to William and Thomas. She hastily rinsed her hands in the bucket of soapy water, following the older girl across the workhouse yard, her heart pounding in her chest.

When she reached Mrs Bell's office, she was met with a sight that made her heart skip a beat. Thomas and William sat huddled together, their eyes wide with fear and surprise. She hadn't seen them in weeks, save for fleeting glimpses during meal times.

She rushed to them, dropping to her knees and pulling them into a tight embrace. "Thomas, William," she breathed out, her voice choked with emotion. They clung to her tightly, their small bodies shaking, the familiar scent of them filling her senses.

But the reunion was cut short by the sharp voice of Mrs Bell. "Enough of that," she snapped, her stern gaze falling on the siblings. "This is not a time for sentimentality."

Reluctantly, Maggie released her brothers, turning her bright blue eyes to the matron, her jaw set with determination. She didn't know why they had been summoned, what new challenge they would face, but she knew one thing for certain. They would overcome it.

Mrs Bell regarded the three children with cold, unfeeling eyes, taking perverse pleasure in the task that lay before her. Her thin lips twisted into a smirk as she casually delivered the news.

"Your mother's dead."

The words hung in the air like a death knell, each syllable echoing in the silence that followed.

"Fell ill, passed away last week. The workhouse has only just been informed," she added dismissively, as if the life and death of their mother was merely another administrative detail.

Thomas' sobs filled the room, his small body trembling violently. William clung to Maggie, his wide eyes filled with confusion and fear. Maggie felt her heart clench at the sight of her brothers, their sorrow striking her like a physical blow.

But she remained outwardly stoic, her blue eyes never leaving Mrs Bell. She struggled to process the news, to accept that their mother was truly gone. This woman, who had chosen a life of luxury over her own children, was no longer part of their world.

Maggie didn't know what to feel. There was a bitter sting of betrayal, a quiet echo of loss, a hollow space where love once lived. But there was also a kernel of doubt that she couldn't shake off.

Could she trust the matron's words? Were they the truth, or yet another cruel trick designed to break their spirits?

Mrs Bell seemed to relish the power her words held, the shock and despair that they provoked. She offered no comfort, no kind words, only a cold, cruel satisfaction at the children's grief.

Tears welled in Maggie's eyes, not for the mother who had abandoned them, but for her brothers who were too young to understand the complexities of their situation. She had to be strong for them.

She drew her brothers closer, whispering soft words of comfort, her voice steady despite the turmoil within her. "It's all right," she murmured, her gaze never leaving Mrs Bell. "We're going to be okay."

She didn't know if it was a promise or a prayer, a plea to a world that had shown them nothing but cruelty. But as she held her brothers close, their bodies wracked with sobs, she knew one thing for certain. She would not let the workhouse break them.

Once Mrs Bell dismissed them with a wave of her hand, as though they were nothing more than a minor inconvenience, the siblings found themselves standing in the austere hallway. The heavy wooden door of the matron's office closed with a definitive thud behind them.

Thomas was still crying, his small shoulders shaking. William was silent, but his lower lip quivered, his eyes glistening with unshed tears.

Maggie, their pillar of strength, took a deep breath, pulling both of them into a tight embrace. "Listen to me, both of you," she started, her voice gentle but firm.

"Will, Tom, look at me," she urged, lifting their chins to meet her eyes. She had to be strong, for them. She had to carry their grief as well as her own.

"I know it's hard," she said, swallowing down her own sadness. "I know it hurts, but do you remember what Papa always said, remember his favourite story?"

"The one about the lion?" Thomas sniffled, his tears leaving clean tracks on his dirt-smudged face.

"That's right," Maggie said, a faint smile playing on her lips. "He said we're like the lion, remember? No matter how hard life gets, we have a lion's heart. We're strong, and we can face anything together."

William sniffed, wiping at his eyes with the back of his hand. "Even without Mama?" he asked, his voice small and shaky.

Maggie nodded, pulling them closer. "Even without Mama. We have each other, and that's more than enough. We're going to stick together, okay?"

It was a promise, a vow of protection and love. And as she held them, her heart ached with the weight of it. She was ready to carry that burden, for them, for the family they still had in each other.

Chapter 3

A year later

The seasons changed, but life within the workhouse remained as grim and harsh as ever. Maggie, now thirteen, had grown stronger, her resolve steeled by the daily trials she and her brothers faced.

It was on a frigid winter day that Maggie was once again summoned by Mrs Bell. A gust of icy wind swept through the workhouse yard as she walked towards the matron's office, her mind filled with apprehension.

Mrs Bell wasted no time in delivering her news. "Miss Pettington, the local seamstress, needs a new employee. You will leave the workhouse and start work for her immediately."

Maggie's heart pounded in her chest, her thoughts racing. Leaving the workhouse meant leaving her brothers. "But, my brothers—" she started, her voice choked with fear.

Mrs Bell cut her off with a wave of her hand. "Your brothers will remain here. They're too young to be sent out."

"I can't leave them," Maggie protested, the mere thought of leaving William and Thomas behind filling her with dread.

For her insubordination, she was met with a swift strike from Mrs Bell's belt, the sharp sting of it echoing her words. "You will do as you are told, girl," Mrs Bell snarled, her eyes gleaming with a cruel satisfaction.

The room spun around Maggie as she grappled with the harsh reality. She would be separated from her brothers. She would not be there to comfort them, to protect them.

Mrs Bell's voice snapped her back to the present. "Now go pack your things. You leave first thing tomorrow."

With a heavy heart, Maggie nodded, biting back tears. She was powerless against the cruel whims of the matron. As she left the office, her mind was consumed with thoughts of her brothers, their fate now out of her hands.

All she could do was promise to find a way back to them, to reunite their small family. She wouldn't allow the workhouse, or Mrs Bell, to sever the bond they shared. She was Maggie Barlow, the big sister with a lion's heart, and she would fight for her brothers, no matter what.

***

Escorted by Mrs Bell, Maggie was led to a small, cramped tenement building that was to be her new home. As she stepped inside, she was greeted by a dimly lit room, the meagre light from a single, grimy window casting long, desolate shadows on the peeling wallpaper. The air smelled of damp and decay, a stark reminder of the countless lives that had been lived, and suffered, within those four walls.

However, amidst the gloom and neglect, signs of care were evident. The threadbare rug had been swept clean, a few faded but carefully tended flowers adorned the small wooden table, and the two narrow beds had been made neatly with what looked like a patchwork of old clothing. The other two girls who shared this room, fellow workhouse children like her, had obviously strived to maintain some semblance of order in their harsh existence.

As she took in her new surroundings, a strange sense of reality settled over her. This was her new home, a world away from her brothers and the familiar hardships of the workhouse. She felt a profound sense of displacement, as though she was a stranger in a strange land, disconnected from everything and everyone she knew.

Mrs Bell's voice cut through her thoughts, her tone as cold and harsh as the winter wind outside. "You'll report to Miss Pettington's shop at midday. Be prompt, or you'll be sent back to the workhouse."

With that, the matron turned on her heel, leaving Maggie standing in the small room, the echo of her words hanging heavy in the silence. The door closed with a deafening thud, leaving her alone with her thoughts.

Maggie took a deep breath, steeling herself against the rush of emotions. Fear, confusion, and worry for her brothers threatened to overwhelm her, but she pushed them down, reminding herself of the promise she had made.

This was just another challenge, another obstacle to overcome. She was

Maggie Barlow, the girl with a lion's heart, and she would not be defeated. She would endure, survive, and find a way back to her brothers.

It was not long before the door creaked open again, this time admitting two girls. One was tall and lanky with a nest of untamed red curls, the other shorter, with mousy brown hair pulled back in a neat bun. They both had the same worn look about them, a tell-tale sign of life in the workhouse. These were her new roommates, Elaine and Dorothy.

Elaine was the first to speak, extending a hand to Maggie. "You must be the new girl. I'm Elaine," she said, her voice surprisingly warm. Dorothy followed suit, a shy smile playing on her lips.

"I'm Dorothy. Welcome, Maggie," she said softly, her eyes, though weary, held a hint of kindness.

Though Maggie was still weighed down by the heartache of leaving her brothers and the bleak prospect of her new life, she couldn't help but feel a small sense of comfort. Elaine and Dorothy were living proof that she could endure this new challenge, just as they had.

She met their extended hands with her own, a silent acknowledgment of the unspoken pact they were forming. In this cramped, dark room, in the heart of this relentless city, they would face their trials together.

"I'm Maggie," she replied, the faintest trace of a smile on her lips.

Despite the hardships she had faced and the uncertainties that lay ahead, she found solace in their presence. They were strangers bound by similar fates, forced to rely on each other in this harsh world.

Chapter 4

In the faint morning light, Maggie sat at the small table, penning a letter to her brothers. Her handwriting was neat and simple, mindful that William was only just beginning to read. She filled the paper with words of hope and promises of a better future, her heartache flowing into every letter. She told them to be brave, to endure, promising she would get them out of the workhouse someday.

With a sigh, she folded the letter and tucked it into a thin envelope. As she scrawled their names across the front, she thought of their innocent faces, wondering if they missed her as much as she missed them.

Maggie left the tenement building with the letter tucked safely in her pocket, heading down the frost-kissed streets of London. It was a tip from Elaine, an overheard conversation, a gossip about a woman who had traded poverty for opulence, that led her to believe her mother might be residing in one of the grand houses that lined the streets. Her heart pounded in her chest as she neared her destination.

The house was everything the workhouse was not - beautiful, elegant, and exuding an air of wealth. Its ornate windows glittered in the morning sun, and the iron gates were grand and imposing. Maggie couldn't help but feel a pang of bitterness. This was where her mother lived, leaving her children to the cold mercy of the workhouse while she enjoyed the comforts of wealth.

Her heart clenched as she stood outside the imposing structure, her gaze trailing over the grand architecture. This was a world her mother had chosen over her own children, a world of affluence and opulence that had won over the love for her family.

A gust of cold wind snapped her out of her bitter reverie, and she turned on her heel, her mind filled with a newfound determination. This was not the life she would choose for her brothers. She would get them out of the workhouse, bring them to a home filled with love, not material wealth.

Taking a deep breath, Maggie rapped her knuckles against the heavy wooden door of the grand house. The sound echoed back at her, amplifying her nervousness. The door creaked open, revealing a well-dressed man.

His demeanour was as cold and austere as the house he resided in.

"I'm looking for Lottie Barlow," Maggie blurted out, her voice steadier than she felt.

"Lottie Barlow..." he repeated slowly, his face dropping, eyes clouding with sorrow. "I'm afraid Lottie passed away over a year ago. The flu, it was."

A chill ran down Maggie's spine, and she tightened her grip on the fabric of her worn-out dress. "Are you sure?" she asked, desperate for him to deny it.

His gaze softened just a tad as he nodded. "Yes, child. Quite sure. It was quite a tragedy. She was a fine lady."

Maggie wanted to scoff at his words, to yell at him about the 'fine lady' who abandoned her children. But she remained silent, pressing her lips into a thin line.

"I... I see. Thank you for your time, sir," she managed to get out, her voice hoarse.

The man simply nodded, offering her a curt, "Good day," before he shut the door in her face.

As Maggie returned to the tenement, she felt an exhaustion that went beyond physical tiredness. She quietly pushed open the creaking door, stepping into the dimly lit room she now called home.

Elaine looked up from the small wooden table where she was mending a pair of socks. Dorothy was sprawled out on one of the thin mattresses, a worn book open on her chest, her eyes closed in sleep. The sight of them, their quiet persistence in the face of hardships, was somehow both heartening and heartbreaking.

"How'd it go?" Elaine asked, setting aside the socks. Her gaze was steady, but Maggie could see the unspoken understanding in her eyes. They were all bound by shared sorrows and silent sufferings.

Maggie sighed, removing her shawl and hanging it on a peg by the door. She hesitated for a moment, her gaze drifting towards the sleeping Dorothy. She didn't want to disrupt the girl's moment of peace. Still, she couldn't keep it to herself. She took a deep breath, her voice barely a whisper, "She's gone. My mother is gone."

Elaine's expression softened, her hand reaching out to offer a comforting squeeze on Maggie's. "I'm sorry, Maggie."

Maggie gave a weak nod, a bitter smile playing on her lips. "I don't know why I'm surprised," she admitted, her gaze falling to her hands. "It's not like she was there for us even when she was alive."

"It was a hope, wasn't it?" Elaine said gently, her voice barely audible. "A hope that maybe one day she'd come back... help you and your brothers."

"Yes," Maggie conceded, her eyes stinging with unshed tears. "It was a hope. A foolish one."

"No hope is foolish, Maggie," Elaine responded, her voice strong yet comforting. "Hope is what keeps us going."

Maggie nodded, touched by Elaine's words. "Now, I just need to figure out how to help my brothers without her."

"You're not alone, Maggie," Elaine said, giving her hand another comforting squeeze. "You have us. And we'll figure it out together."

As she listened to Elaine's encouraging words, Maggie felt a glimmer of hope. She may have lost a mother, but she had found a family in these girls. They were her strength, her solace in this harsh world. And together, they would find a way to make things better. She had a promise to keep, and with her newfound family by her side, she felt ready to face whatever came next.

Chapter 5

Four years later

Four long years had passed since Maggie had first been assigned to the seamstress' shop. Each week, she'd been returning to the workhouse, desperate for a glimpse of her brothers. Each time, she had been met with Mrs Bell's cold refusal.

As Maggie stepped into the workhouse once more, her heart pounding in her chest, the sense of dread was as potent as it was familiar. The narrow corridors echoed with the ghostly whispers of her past, the shared rooms filled with silent, miserable children reminding her of the life she had once led.

Mrs Bell sat behind her desk, her stern face impassive as Maggie was led into the room. The matron's cruel eyes scrutinised Maggie, as if she were still that desperate little girl who had first arrived at the workhouse four years ago.

"You're here again, Barlow?" Mrs Bell's voice sliced through the tense silence, a hint of derision in her tone.

Maggie clenched her fists, steeling herself. "I'm here to see my brothers," she replied, her voice as steady as she could manage.

"I'm afraid that won't be possible," Mrs Bell stated flatly, not meeting her gaze.

Maggie felt as if the ground had been ripped from beneath her feet. "You say that every week. Why do I feel like you mean something different today?" she demanded, her heart pounding.

"They've been sent away," the matron replied, the satisfaction in her voice impossible to miss.

"Sent away? Where?" Maggie took a step forward, her mind spinning with questions and fears.

"To a factory. An apprentice opportunity. A chance for them to learn a trade, make something of themselves."

"Where? Which factory?" Maggie asked, desperation creeping into her voice.

The matron shrugged nonchalantly, as if the destiny of the two boys was of no consequence to her. "I don't see why that's any of your concern. They are workhouse children, after all. They're better off."

"They're my brothers!" Maggie shouted, her heart pounding in her chest.

"And what of it?" Mrs Bell retorted coldly, her gaze finally meeting Maggie's. "You're no longer their caretaker, Barlow. They're under the jurisdiction of the workhouse now."

"But..."

"No buts, Barlow. You've no right to know," the matron cut her off, standing from her desk, her decision final. "Now leave, before I have you escorted out."

As Maggie was pushed out of the office, she felt a despair she hadn't felt in years. Her brothers, Thomas and William, had been whisked away without her knowledge, without even a chance for her to say goodbye.

Maggie moved through the dismal halls of the workhouse, her mind a whirl of fear and desperation. Spotting a worker - a young woman with a weary face - she rushed over, barely containing her panic.

"Do you know my brothers? Thomas and William Barlow?" Maggie asked urgently, her gaze pleading.

"I'm... I'm sorry. I just started here last month, I don't know them," the worker replied, her eyes wide with surprise.

Frustration surged within Maggie and she snapped, "How can you not know? They've been here for years!"

The worker recoiled, her face paling, and Maggie immediately regretted her outburst. It wasn't this poor girl's fault. "I'm sorry," she said, her voice softening. "I didn't mean to... I'm just worried."

"I understand," the worker murmured, her gaze sympathetic. "I'm sorry I couldn't help."

Maggie nodded, biting her lip to keep the tears at bay. She hurried down the hallway, stopping another, older, worker. "Do you know where Thomas and William Barlow were sent? Please, they're my brothers."

"I'm sorry, Miss," the worker replied, shaking her head. "I don't know. The matron handles all the placements."

Maggie's heart sank, a chill creeping into her veins. It felt like a nightmare that she couldn't wake from. Everywhere she turned, she was met with the same response - no one knew where her brothers were.

"Thank you," she muttered to the worker, her voice hollow. She turned away, wrapping her arms around herself as she stared down the bleak corridors of the workhouse. It was as if her brothers had vanished into thin air, swallowed by the cruel system they'd been entrapped in.

Maggie lingered in the shadows of the grim corridor, her heart pounding in her chest. As soon as the last of the workers disappeared, she slipped into the courtyard. Her breath hitched as the familiar sight of the courtyard washed over her. It was a vivid flashback to her own workhouse days, a time she'd tried so hard to escape, both physically and emotionally.

The long stone benches lined with laundry tubs, the sheets of white fabric billowing in the breeze, and the constant sound of scrubbing and wringing filled the air. It was all exactly the same, a haunting tableau of the past she had left behind. The only change was the faces – young, old, worn out by hardships and the relentless passage of time.

Keeping her head down so as not to attract attention, she approached the line of women hunched over the wash basins. She recognised a few from her own time there, their faces hardened but not unkind. She approached one of them, a woman with greying hair and calloused hands, scrubbing diligently at a stubborn stain.

"Excuse me," Maggie murmured, her voice barely audible over the sounds of the yard. The woman paused, looking up to meet her gaze. "I'm looking for my brothers, Thomas and William Barlow. Do you know them?"

The woman squinted at Maggie for a moment before shaking her head. "Sorry, dear. There are so many children here, it's hard to keep track."

Maggie nodded, trying to mask her disappointment. She moved to the next woman, asking the same question, receiving the same answer. Her heart sank a little more with each negative response.

With each denial, the reality of her brothers' absence became more pronounced, their presence in the workhouse washed away like stains from the clothes in the basins. As she turned away from the last woman, she glanced around the courtyard once more, the feeling of despair lingering in the air.

In the harsh reality of the workhouse, her brothers had been just two more faces among the crowd. Now, they were gone, their existence wiped clean, leaving only Maggie to remember and seek them. And she would, until she found them. The determination pulsed through her veins like a heartbeat, echoing her unspoken promise – she would find her brothers, and bring them home.

As Maggie was about to step out of the courtyard, a shadow fell across her path. She looked up, her gaze colliding with a familiar face.

Maggie's heart stuttered in her chest. The woman turned towards her, and recognition bloomed on her face. It was Sally, a fellow inmate from Maggie's days at the workhouse.

"Maggie?" Sally's voice echoed with surprise. "Is that really you?"

Maggie nodded, biting her lower lip, her mind racing with renewed hope. "Yes, it's me. Sally, you wouldn't happen to remember my brothers, would you? Thomas and William?"

Sally's brow furrowed, a wrinkle of deep thought appearing between her brows. "Thomas and William Barlow, you mean?"

Maggie's heart jumped at the familiar surnames, her own. "Yes! Yes, that's them."

Sally's expression shifted into one of regret. "Oh, Maggie, I'm sorry, but they left last Tuesday. They were sent off with a group of boys."

Despair threatened to pull Maggie under once more, but she fought against it. "Do you... do you know where?"

Sally shook her head, a remorseful look in her eyes. "No, Maggie. They don't tell us where they send the children."

Maggie nodded, her heart heavy with the cold reality of their situation. Yet, as she turned to leave, Sally added, "although, my cousin Christopher was among them. I don't know if that helps, but it's all I know."

Maggie turned back, her eyes wide. A lead. It was a slim one, but it was something. Her heart clenched at the shred of hope. "Thank you, Sally," she whispered, her voice thick with unshed tears. "Thank you so much."

As she walked away from the courtyard, the glimmer of hope sparked a renewed determination within her. She had a lead, a direction to focus her search. She was not powerless. Christopher, Sally's cousin, had been taken with her brothers.

She would follow this thread of hope, no matter how thin or fragile. She would find her brothers and bring them home. This was her mission, her responsibility, her purpose. And Maggie Barlow was nothing if not determined.

As Maggie began the long walk back to her tenement, her thoughts swirled around her brothers. Where were they now? Were they safe? The questions gnawed at her, casting a shadow over the faint hope she clung to. Were they being treated better at the factory than the workhouse? She hoped so, prayed so. Every step homeward echoed with the rhythm of her worries.

When she finally arrived at the humble dwelling she shared with Elaine and Dorothy, her heart was heavy and her steps weary. Yet, as she pushed open the door, the warmth of the small room engulfed her. Elaine and Dorothy looked up from their sewing, their faces softening with concern.

"Maggie, dear, what's wrong?" Elaine asked, rising to her feet. Dorothy's eyes, too, were filled with worry.

Maggie bit back the tears, her throat tight. "I... I found out about my brothers," she managed to say. "They're gone. Moved off to some factory." She then recounted the conversation with Sally, the lead she'd been given, and her worries for her brothers.

As she spoke, Elaine and Dorothy listened, their faces mirroring Maggie's own concern. They had become more than just housemates over the past four years. They had become her sisters, sharing in her joys, her fears, and her dreams.

"I'm so sorry, Maggie," Elaine murmured, wrapping an arm around her. Dorothy reached for her hand, offering silent support. Maggie felt the tears well up in her eyes, but this time, they were tears of gratitude. She was not alone in this struggle. She had Elaine and Dorothy by her side.

They were her family now, just as much as her brothers were. Together, they had faced the hardships of life, weathering the storms with a resilience born out of shared experiences. They had shared laughter, tears, and dreams. They had woven a tapestry of sisterhood that transcended the confines of their cramped tenement.

Maggie drew strength from their presence, their unwavering support providing a salve to her troubled heart. She was not alone in this battle. She had her sisters. And with their support, she would face the daunting task ahead.

She would find her brothers. She had to. For them, and for the newfound family she had found in Elaine and Dorothy. No matter what the future held, they would face it together. And for now, that was enough.

Chapter 6

A year had passed since Maggie's last lead on her brothers had turned out to be a dead end. Each day since, her heart ached a bit more, each unanswered question adding to her burden.

Early in the evening, she found herself at the dressmaker's, the hum of the sewing machine her only company. The fine silk dress she was working on was for a wealthy lady, a far cry from the rough garments of the workhouse. Yet, the comfort it promised only emphasised the distance between her and her brothers.

As she expertly guided the fabric under the needle, her mind was miles away. She thought of William and Thomas, of their smiles and their laughter, and of the bond they shared. She wondered what they looked like now. Would she recognise them if she saw them on the street?

Her heart ached at the thought. A year of searching, of hoping, of dreaming, and yet she felt no closer to finding them. Was it futile? Would she ever see them again?

She glanced at the clock on the wall. Eight o'clock. She sighed, shaking off her thoughts. The dress was almost finished, but it would have to wait until the morning. She packed her tools, shut down the sewing machine, and turned off the lights. The shop turned into a pool of shadows, a mirror of her heavy heart.

Stepping outside, the cool night air caressed her face, offering a moment of peace. But it was short-lived. As she started her journey home, a figure lurched out of the shadows.

A sailor, reeking of alcohol, barred her path. His glassy eyes leered at her, his grin wide and disturbing. A shiver of fear shot down her spine. Maggie's heart pounded in her chest. The deserted street offered no help, no escape. It was just her, the drunk sailor, and the long night stretching out before her.

"Ain't you a pretty sight?" the sailor slurred, his words coated in alcohol and malice. His grin widened, revealing yellowed teeth. Maggie recoiled at the sight and the sour smell of his breath, her heart pounding even harder in her chest.

"Please, let me go," Maggie said, her voice steadier than she felt. The man only laughed in response, the sound echoing around the empty street, a chilling reminder of their solitude.

"I ain't done with you yet," he growled, reaching out and grabbing her by the arm. Maggie flinched at his touch, the rough callouses on his hand a sharp contrast to the delicate fabric she'd been working with only moments ago. She tried to pull away, but his grip was like iron.

"I have no money," Maggie protested, her mind racing. Her voice wavered slightly, betraying her fear, but she forced herself to meet his gaze. She couldn't afford to show weakness, not now.

The man sneered at her response, his bloodshot eyes narrowing in suspicion. "You work in that fancy dressmaker's, don't you? Don't lie to me, girl!"

"I work for wages, but I don't have any money on me," Maggie insisted, desperately trying to pull her arm free. But his grip only tightened, a vice around her wrist.

His laughter was harsh, a mocking echo that bounced off the cobblestones and into the night. The desperation in Maggie's eyes seemed to amuse him, but his amusement was tinged with frustration. "You're lying," he spat out, his grip on her arm tightening.

"I'm not!" Maggie gasped, wincing at the pain shooting up her arm. She tried again to free herself, but the man was unyielding. She scanned the surroundings for an escape, but the deserted street offered no help. The only light came from a distant street lamp, casting long, menacing shadows. All around them, the shops and houses stood silent, their shutters drawn and their occupants oblivious to her plight.

The fear was a heavy stone in her stomach, her mind filled with thoughts of her brothers, her friends, and the life she had been trying so hard to build. She couldn't let this man ruin it all. She wouldn't. She was a Barlow, after all, and Barlows were fighters.

Gathering her courage, Maggie drew back her free hand and, with all her strength, struck the man across the jaw. His head snapped back, the shock breaking his vice-like grip on her arm.

"I said, let me go!" she shouted, her voice ringing out in the silence of the night. But the victory was fleeting. The impact had surprised him, but it only seemed to enrage him further.

"What the--!" he roared, a hand flying to his cheek. His eyes blazed in the dim light, his drunken stupor replaced by a vicious anger. Before Maggie could run, he lunged forward, catching her off guard. His rough hand seized her shoulder, and with a grunt of effort, he flung her to the cobblestone ground.

Pain shot through her body as she hit the cold, hard ground. Her breath hitched in her chest, and for a moment, everything seemed to spin. She could hear the man's laughter, a chilling sound that echoed off the stone walls around them.

"You think you can hit me and run, do you?" he sneered, towering over her. His voice echoed in the quiet street, his words bouncing off the stone buildings around them. He didn't seem to care who heard, his anger and humiliation overshadowing his earlier caution.

Maggie pushed herself onto her elbows, her body protesting each movement. But she couldn't afford to stay down. Not when her freedom was at stake. Not when her brothers still needed her.

Ignoring the pain, she pushed herself up to her knees. She met the man's glare with a defiant stare of her own. She was bruised and battered, but she wasn't beaten. Not yet.

The night stretched on, the solitary street lamp casting an eerie glow on the scene.

The distant hoot of an owl was the only sound breaking the tense silence. Maggie steeled herself for the next round, her resolve unwavering. This was a fight she couldn't afford to lose. She had too much at stake. Too much to lose.

With renewed determination, she rose to her feet. She saw three people walking towards her, but they stopped and kept their distance from her, not wanting to get involved.

As Maggie readied herself for the inevitable confrontation, a figure emerged from the gloom. He was young, his face just losing the soft edges of boyhood, but his eyes were warm and concerned. A gentle smile touched his lips, an oasis of kindness in an otherwise bleak situation.

He didn't speak, but there was a determination in his gaze that spoke volumes. He stepped between Maggie and the sailor, his slight frame casting an unlikely barrier. His hands were raised in a gesture of peace, but the look in his eyes was far from serene.

"Leave her be," he said, his voice steady. His words seemed to hang in the air, an echo of decency in the midst of the turmoil. The sailor turned his attention to the newcomer, his eyes narrowing in confusion and then growing wide with anger.

But before he could react, the boy darted toward Maggie, his intention clear. The sailor made one last lunge, his fist flying toward her. Maggie saw it coming, but it was too late to dodge. She felt the sting of the blow across her cheek, a searing pain that shot through her body. Her vision blurred, and a numbness began to creep into her limbs.

The world spun around her as she slumped to the ground, the cobblestones cold against her cheek. She could hear a distant struggle, a muffled shouting that seemed to fade in and out. But her consciousness was ebbing, the world growing darker by the second.

She caught one last glimpse of the boy, his brown eyes wide with fear, before darkness claimed her. He was rushing towards her, his arms reaching out. But it was too late. The world tipped on its axis, and she surrendered to the inevitable oblivion.

As she slipped into unconsciousness, her last thought was of her brothers. Of William and Thomas, of their shared dreams and secret hopes. And of her promise, one she had not yet fulfilled.

In her dreams, she saw their faces. Two pairs of bright blue eyes, so like her own, filled with courage and hope. Their memory was a beacon in the darkness, guiding her, reminding her of what she was fighting for.

Maggie let the darkness take her.

Chapter 7

Interlude; Luke, seven years ago

Luke stood nervously at the entrance to the bustling docks, his threadbare clothes a stark contrast to the elegant attire worn by the nobility he secretly belonged to. He took a deep breath, steeling himself for the encounter ahead, and approached the dock master's office.

Pushing open the heavy wooden door, Luke found himself face-to-face with Joseph Darby, the stern and weathered dock master. Joseph looked up from his desk, his eyes narrowing as they landed on the young man standing before him.

"What brings you here, lad?" Joseph's voice held a gruffness that matched his appearance.

Luke cleared his throat, his voice betraying a hint of nervousness. "Sir, my name is Luke. I... I'm looking for work. I heard you might have some openings here."

Joseph's gaze travelled up and down Luke's form, taking in his worn-out shoes and patched-up trousers. He sighed and shook his head. "We've got enough hands already. Can't be taking on every stray that comes by."

Luke's heart sank, but he refused to give up. "Please, sir, I'm a hard worker. I'll do whatever you need. I just need a chance."

Joseph's face softened slightly as he regarded the determined young man. He grumbled under his breath before motioning for Luke to take a seat.

"Fine, sit down. But I ain't making any promises. You better have a good reason for bothering me, lad," Joseph said, his tone still gruff but with a trace of curiosity.

Luke sat down, grateful for the opportunity to state his case. "Thank you, sir. You see, my… my father is a nobleman, but he won't have anything to do with me. My mother is gone now, I have to take care of myself."

Joseph leaned back in his chair, his eyes fixed on Luke as he listened intently. "So, you're telling me you come from the upper crust? And you want to work here, with the common folk?"

Luke nodded earnestly. "Yes, sir. I want to prove myself, to show that I'm more than just a name. I want to earn an honest living."

Joseph's demeanour softened further, his gaze now filled with understanding. "You know, lad, life ain't easy for any of us. The docks can be a harsh place. But I respect someone who's willing to work hard and make their own way."

Luke's face brightened with a glimmer of hope. "I'll work twice as hard as anyone else, sir. I promise you won't regret giving me a chance."

Joseph leaned forward, a rare hint of warmth in his eyes. "All right, Luke. I'll give you a shot. Just don't expect any special treatment. You'll start at the bottom like everyone else, and you'll have to prove yourself every step of the way."

Luke nodded eagerly, gratitude evident on his face. "Thank you, sir. You won't regret this. I'll do my best, I promise."

As Joseph watched Luke's genuine enthusiasm, he couldn't help but feel a sense of admiration for the young man. "We'll see, lad. We'll see. Now, let's get you some work clothes. You'll start first thing tomorrow."

***

The next morning, as the sun began to rise over the docks, Luke eagerly awaited Joseph Darby's arrival. Clad in his new work clothes, he felt a renewed sense of purpose. When Joseph finally emerged from his office, Luke hurried to catch up with him.

"Good morning, sir," Luke greeted with a respectful nod. "I'm ready to learn."

Joseph looked at Luke, studying his eager expression, and nodded approvingly. "We'll start with the basics, lad. Come with me."

Luke followed Joseph as they weaved their way through the bustling dockyard. The air was filled with the sounds of seagulls, creaking ships, and the distant shouts of workers. Luke marvelled at the organised chaos, taking in the sights and sounds with wide-eyed fascination.

Joseph led him to a group of dockworkers loading crates onto a ship. "Pay attention, Luke. This is how it's done."

Luke watched intently as the workers moved heavy crates with practiced precision. His sharp eyes followed their movements, quickly absorbing the techniques they employed. Before long, he couldn't contain his curiosity.

"Sir, may I try?" Luke asked, his enthusiasm bubbling over.

Joseph hesitated for a moment, assessing Luke's eagerness, before nodding. "Give it a go, lad. But be careful."

Luke stepped forward, his muscles tense with anticipation. He studied the workers' methods once more, mimicking their actions as best he could. With a surge of determination, he lifted a smaller crate, his strength surprising even himself. Sweat trickled down his brow as he carefully carried it towards the ship.

Joseph observed Luke's movements, his eyes widening in surprise. "Not bad, lad. You're a quick learner."

Encouraged by Joseph's words, Luke's confidence soared. He eagerly took on more tasks, from loading crates to securing ropes, always striving to improve. Joseph watched in amazement as Luke adapted to each task with remarkable speed.

"You've got a natural knack for this, Luke," Joseph commented, a note of admiration in his voice. "Most people take weeks to learn what you've picked up in a day."

A broad smile spread across Luke's face, pride swelling within him. "Thank you, sir. I'm grateful for this opportunity."

As the day progressed, Luke continued to impress, his enthusiasm shining through his every action. Joseph took note of his dedication, gradually warming up to him as they conversed about life, dreams, and the hardships they had both faced.

At the end of the day, Joseph turned to Luke, his eyes filled with genuine respect. "You've surpassed my expectations, lad. I've seen many come and go, but few with your determination. You've earned my respect."

Luke's heart swelled with gratitude. "Thank you, sir. I won't let you down. I'll continue to work hard every day."

Joseph clapped a hand on Luke's shoulder, a rare display of warmth. "I believe you, Luke. Keep that fire in you, and you'll go far in this world."

Luke smiled, feeling a sense of belonging he had never experienced before.

As the sun dipped below the horizon two weeks later, casting a warm glow over the docks, Luke and Joseph found themselves standing by the water's edge, the sound of lapping waves filling the air.

Joseph turned to Luke, his eyes filled with a mix of admiration and paternal affection. "Luke, there's something different about you. You have the potential to go far in this career, should you choose it."

Luke's heart swelled with pride and a bittersweet longing. He had never received such genuine praise, especially from someone he respected. The unspoken words between them resonated deeply, and for a fleeting moment, Luke wondered if this was what it felt like to have a father—a kind, guiding presence in his life.

"Thank you, sir," Luke managed to say, his voice tinged with emotion. "Your words mean more to me than you can imagine. To have your faith in me, it's... it's something I've longed for."

Joseph's gruff exterior softened further, and he placed a hand on Luke's shoulder, offering a comforting squeeze. "You've earned every bit of it, Luke. Never forget that.

Your past doesn't define you; it's your character and your actions that matter."

Luke nodded, his eyes glistening with unshed tears. The weight of his past burdens seemed to ease as he stood beside Joseph, a man who believed in him when no one else had. In that tender moment, a bond formed between them, one that surpassed the confines of mentorship.

A small smile played on Luke's lips as he absorbed Joseph's words, realising that family was not solely defined by blood but by the connections that are forged along life's path. In Joseph, he had found a guiding light—a mentor, a friend, and perhaps something even deeper.

As the dock lights flickered to life, Luke and Joseph turned their gaze toward the future, united by a shared purpose and a bond that transcended societal boundaries. The docks had become more than just a workplace; they had become a haven where dreams were nurtured, and a sense of belonging was finally discovered.

As Luke climbed into his modest bed that evening, exhaustion mingled with a newfound sense of purpose. The flickering candle cast dancing shadows on the worn walls, as his thoughts swirled with anticipation and determination.

The loss of his mother weighed heavy on his heart, but now, more than ever, he felt an unyielding drive to honour her memory. The docks had become his sanctuary, and through his hard work and dedication, he hoped to create a better life for himself and prove that he was more than the circumstances of his birth.

Gazing out of the small window, Luke caught a glimpse of the starry sky. The shimmering constellations seemed to whisper to him, promising a future filled with possibilities. He closed his eyes, picturing his mother's face, and whispered, "I will make you proud, Mother. I will rise above the limitations imposed upon me."

With each passing day, Luke's resolve strengthened. He awoke each morning with renewed vigour, ready to face the challenges that awaited him at the docks. His fellow workers had become his surrogate family, and he was grateful for their camaraderie and support.

Luke's hands, once calloused and rough, now bore the marks of honest labour. The physical toil had transformed him, shaping him into a man of resilience and fortitude. He knew he still had much to learn, but his thirst for knowledge and his eagerness to prove himself were unwavering.

In the evenings, Luke would find solace in the pages of books borrowed from a kind dockworker. He devoured tales of adventure, wisdom, and knowledge, expanding his horizons beyond the shores of his mundane existence. Each word he absorbed was a step toward unlocking his full potential and reshaping his destiny.

As the days turned into weeks, and the weeks into months, Luke's dedication and skill earned him the respect of his peers and the admiration of Joseph Darby. Their bond deepened, evolving into a mentorship that surpassed the boundaries of their roles. Joseph saw in Luke the promise of a remarkable future, and he encouraged him to pursue his dreams with unwavering support.

And it was one month later when Luke left the heavy physical demands of working at the docks and started working as a clerk in Mr Darby's warehouse by the docks. Grateful to be off the docks, Luke knew he could never repay Mr Darby for his faith in him. If Mr Darby hadn't taken Luke under his wing, Luke shuddered to think where he would be now.

Chapter 8

Luke, now

Luke sat on a weathered bench in the park, watching as his daughter, Charlotte, played amidst a backdrop of vibrant flowers and children's laughter. Her rich brown eyes sparkled with youthful joy, mirroring his own, while her warm-toned skin reflected their shared heritage. It was in these moments, as he witnessed her innocence and spirit, that Luke's heart overflowed with love and pride.

Beside him, Esther, a kind-hearted woman he had been courting, observed Charlotte with a tender smile. She saw the undeniable bond between father and daughter, and her own affection for Charlotte grew with each passing day. Luke had become a beacon of light in her life, and she yearned for a future where they could be a family.

Luke stole a glance at Esther, admiring her grace and compassion. He cherished the moments they had spent together, sharing stories and dreams. But there was a conflict deep within him, a weight that tugged at his heartstrings. He believed that Charlotte needed a mother figure, someone to fill the void left by her late mother. And yet, he couldn't ignore his daughter's hesitance and protective nature.

As Charlotte giggled and twirled around, her innocent eyes caught Esther's gaze. Esther reached out a hand, inviting Charlotte to join them on the bench. "Would you like to sit with us, Charlotte?"

Charlotte hesitated, her small brow furrowing. She glanced at her father, seeking his reassurance. Luke smiled warmly, giving her an encouraging nod.

"It's all right, sweetheart. Esther is a good friend. She cares about both of us," Luke whispered, his voice laced with tenderness.

Reluctantly, Charlotte took Esther's hand and settled next to her on the bench. Esther gently brushed a strand of hair away from Charlotte's face, her eyes brimming with affection. "You're such a special little girl, Charlotte. Your father is lucky to have you."

Charlotte's gaze softened, a mixture of curiosity and wariness evident in her eyes. "Are you going to be my new mommy?"

Esther's heart skipped a beat, and she reached out to hold Charlotte's hand. "I would like to be, Charlotte, but only if you want me to. I would never try to replace your mommy. She will always hold a special place in your heart."

Charlotte pondered Esther's words, her expression pensive. She leaned against Luke, seeking his comforting presence. "I miss Mama. I don't want someone new. I just want Papa."

Luke's heart ached at his daughter's words, torn between his own longing for companionship and his deep understanding of Charlotte's feelings. He wrapped his arm around her, holding her close.

"I understand, Charlotte. I miss Mama too. Esther is not here to replace her. She's here because she cares about us. We can take things slowly, and you can decide if you're comfortable with her being a part of our lives."

Esther nodded, her eyes shimmering with understanding. "I promise, Charlotte, I will always respect your feelings. I will be here as a friend first, someone you can trust and rely on."

As the sun dipped below the horizon, casting a warm glow over the park, Luke felt a mixture of gratitude and unease. He appreciated Esther's understanding and patience, but the lingering question of why Charlotte seemed to resist their connection troubled him. Was it simply the void left by her mother's absence, or was there something more?

The air grew cooler as evening settled in, and Luke offered to walk Esther home, a gesture of chivalry ingrained in his nature. Charlotte, sensing her father's attention shifting, became restless, her steps growing more defiant as they made their way through the dimly lit streets.

Luke tightened his grip on Charlotte's hand, trying to maintain a sense of order despite her resistance. "Charlotte, please, behave yourself. Esther is our guest, and we need to be courteous."

Charlotte's eyes welled with tears, her small voice quivering. "I don't like her, Papa. She's not Mama."

Luke's heart sank at his daughter's words, and he paused, crouching down to her level. "I know it's hard, sweetheart. Esther isn't trying to replace Mama. She just wants to be a friend to us. Can you try to understand that?"

Charlotte's bottom lip quivered, but she nodded, albeit reluctantly. Luke knew it would take time for her wounds to heal, and he resolved to be patient and understanding as she adjusted to the changes in their lives.

They resumed their walk, the tension in the air slowly dissipating as Luke continued to engage in light-hearted conversation with Esther. He admired her strength and resilience, how she remained by his side despite Charlotte's resistance. It deepened his admiration for her, and he couldn't help but feel a glimmer of hope for their future together.

As they reached Esther's doorstep, Luke turned to her, a gentle smile on his face. "Thank you for joining us today, Esther. Despite the challenges, I hope you had some enjoyment."

Esther returned his smile, her eyes filled with understanding and warmth. "Luke, I'm grateful for every moment spent with you and Charlotte. It's not easy, but I believe in us. We can build something beautiful, together."

Luke's heart swelled at Esther's words, her unwavering belief in their potential. He reached out, taking her hand in his, feeling a sense of connection and comfort. "Goodnight, Esther. Rest well, and thank you for your patience and understanding."

Esther squeezed his hand gently, her touch conveying reassurance and support.

"Goodnight, Luke. Take care of yourself and Charlotte. I'll see you soon."

Luke watched as Esther disappeared into her home, a newfound sense of determination coursing through his veins. He knew the road ahead would be challenging, but he was determined to create a loving and nurturing environment for Charlotte while honouring the memory of her mother.

He and Charlotte walked home alone, comfortable silence enveloping them. When they reached his modest house, he carried Charlotte to her upstairs bedroom.

Luke gently tucked Charlotte into bed, making sure she was comfortable and safe. She snuggled under the covers, her eyelids heavy with exhaustion. As he leaned in to plant a soft kiss on her forehead, a sinking feeling struck him. He had forgotten Charlotte's beloved doll at the park.

The thought of leaving his daughter alone made him hesitant, but he knew he couldn't bear to see the disappointment on her face when she woke up without her cherished toy. Luke sighed, knowing he had to retrieve it. He approached Charlotte's bedside, brushing a stray strand of hair from her face.

"Charlotte, my dear, I forgot something very important at the park. I need to go back and get it," Luke explained, his voice laced with regret.

Charlotte stirred, her eyes fluttering open. "Papa, please don't leave me. I don't want to be alone."

Luke's heart ached at his daughter's plea, but he reassured her gently. "I promise, Charlotte, I won't be gone long. Mrs Yates will keep an eye on you until I return. You'll be safe."

Charlotte's tired eyes searched Luke's face, searching for any sign of uncertainty. With a small nod, she mustered a sleepy smile. "All right, Papa. Please come back soon."

Luke pressed a kiss to her forehead once more, his voice filled with tenderness. "I'll be back before you know it, my darling. Sleep well."

With a heavy heart, Luke left Charlotte's room and made his way down the creaking staircase of their home. He knocked gently on Mrs Yates' door, his trusted housekeeper who had shown kindness to both him and Charlotte in the past.

"Mrs Yates, would you mind keeping an eye on Charlotte for a short while? I need to fetch something from the park," Luke requested, his voice a mix of urgency and gratitude.

Mrs Yates, a middle-aged woman with a warm smile, opened the door and nodded empathetically. "Of course, Mr Axton. You can count on me. I'll make sure she's safe and sound until you return."

Relieved, Luke thanked Mrs Yates and hurriedly made his way back to the park. The gas lamps cast an eerie glow on the cobblestone streets, their flickering light creating dancing shadows. Luke's footsteps quickened as he retraced his path, determined to find the doll that held so much significance for Charlotte.

Upon reaching the park, Luke's heart sank as he realised the doll was nowhere to be found. He searched frantically, scouring every nook and cranny, but it seemed to have vanished. A heavy sigh escaped his lips, a mixture of disappointment and concern for Charlotte's reaction.

Resigned to his inability to retrieve the cherished toy, Luke made his way back home, his steps heavy with a sense of defeat. As he walked, lost in his own thoughts, his attention was abruptly pulled away by a commotion near a nearby seamstress shop.

A group of onlookers had gathered, their murmurs and gasps filling the air. Luke's eyes locked onto the scene, and his heart raced with a mixture of instinct and concern. A drunken sailor towered over a young woman with black hair, his aggression escalating.

Without hesitation, Luke rushed forward, interposing himself between the sailor and the defenceless girl. "That's enough!" he commanded, his voice firm and commanding.

The sailor, caught off guard, stumbled backward, his alcohol-fuelled bravado fading momentarily. However, his anger quickly resurfaced, and he swung his fist at Luke with a wild, drunken rage.

Luke's reflexes kicked in, honed from years of physical labour at the docks. He deftly sidestepped the sailor's punch, using his position as a trusted friend of the dock master to his advantage.

"Stand down!" Luke's voice carried authority, as he unleashed the weight of his connection to Joseph Darby. "I suggest you leave this young lady alone, or you'll be facing consequences far beyond what you can handle."

The sailor's eyes widened, a mix of fear and realisation crossing his face. Realising he had met his match, he stumbled away, disappearing into the darkness.

With the immediate threat gone, Luke's attention turned to the young woman who had fallen unconscious from the impact of the sailor's blow. He knelt down beside her, worry etching lines on his forehead.

Cradling the unconscious woman gently in his arms, Luke's worry deepened as he realised she showed no signs of waking. The weight of responsibility pressed upon him, knowing he couldn't leave her there in such a vulnerable state. Determination etched into his features, he resolved to take her home and provide the care she desperately needed.

As Luke carried the woman in his arms, his strides purposeful yet careful, he navigated the familiar streets towards his humble abode. Thoughts of Charlotte's well-being intertwined with concerns for the young woman's health, creating a tapestry of emotions within him.

Upon reaching his home, Luke entered with a soft yet steady step, careful not to disturb Charlotte's slumber. The woman's body felt fragile against his, urging him to find a safe place to lay her down.

He gently settled her onto his own bed, a place of warmth and solace he had reserved for his daughter's comfort. Luke retrieved a basin of cool water and a soft cloth, dampening it before placing it gently on the woman's forehead. He hoped the coolness would offer some relief and aid in her recovery.

He hurriedly retrieved a notebook and pen from a nearby drawer, writing a brief note explaining the situation and requesting a doctor's assistance. He handed it to Mrs Yates, who had kept watch over Charlotte earlier, and requested her assistance in seeking medical aid.

"Mrs Yates, please take this note to Doctor Simmons at the corner clinic. Explain the situation, and kindly ask if he could provide his expertise as soon as possible," Luke implored, his voice laced with urgency.

Mrs Yates nodded, understanding the gravity of the situation. "Don't worry, Mr Luke. I'll make sure this gets to him promptly. We'll do everything we can to help."

Luke breathed a sigh of relief, grateful for Mrs Yates' support. He returned to the young woman's side, ensuring her comfort and well-being. The soft glow of candlelight cast a tranquil ambiance in the room, as Luke sat by her side, keeping a vigilant watch.

In the stillness of the night, his thoughts wandered to Charlotte. He silently prayed that his daughter would remain undisturbed by the events unfolding around her. His paternal instincts tugged at his heart, yearning to protect both his daughter and this stranger in need.

As the minutes ticked by, Luke focused on the rhythmic rise and fall of the woman's chest, finding solace in the steady presence of life. He whispered words of comfort and hope, a silent plea for her swift recovery.

Time seemed to stretch, as the night pressed on and the weight of exhaustion settled upon Luke's shoulders. The flickering candle cast long shadows in the room, dancing with the delicate breaths of the sleeping woman.

In the hushed silence, a glimmer of hope stirred within him, intertwining his fate with hers. Luke knew that whatever the outcome, he had acted out of compassion and a sense of duty. And as he sat there, holding vigil for a stranger, his spirit remained resolute in its dedication to protect those in need, even when it demanded sacrifice.

Chapter 9

A soft knock resounded through the small dwelling, drawing Luke's attention from the young woman's bedside. He swiftly rose to his feet and opened the door to reveal Doctor Simmons, a seasoned physician known for his compassionate care.

"Doctor Simmons, thank you for coming," Luke greeted, his voice laced with relief and concern. "Please, come in. She's in here."

The doctor nodded and followed Luke into the dimly lit room. His experienced eyes scanned the woman's still form, his brow furrowing with concern. Luke stood nearby, his posture tense, his worry apparent in his every fibre.

Doctor Simmons carefully approached the bed, his voice calm yet inquisitive. "What happened to her? Can you provide any information about her condition?"

Luke swallowed hard, his voice tinged with apprehension. "I found her being assaulted by a drunken sailor. I intervened, but she was struck and fell unconscious. I brought her here, hoping you could help."

The doctor's eyes narrowed as he listened, his focus shifting between Luke and the woman lying before him. He reached out to gently touch her wrist, feeling for her pulse. "You did the right thing by bringing her here. Let me examine her and determine the extent of her injuries."

Luke nodded, his gaze fixed on the doctor's every movement. The room seemed to grow smaller, suffused with the anticipation of the unknown. He took a step back, allowing Doctor Simmons to conduct his examination.

Time seemed to slow as Luke anxiously waited outside the bedroom door, his heart heavy with concern for the young woman's well-being. He clasped his hands together, his mind flooded with a whirlwind of thoughts and prayers.

The muffled sounds of the doctor's careful ministrations echoed from within, followed by brief moments of silence that seemed to stretch into an eternity. Each passing second intensified the weight of uncertainty, and Luke longed for the reassurance of hopeful news.

Finally, the bedroom door creaked open, and Doctor Simmons emerged, his expression thoughtful. He met Luke's gaze, his voice measured yet compassionate. "Luke, she has suffered a blow to the head, resulting in a possible concussion. It will take time for her to recover fully."

Relief washed over Luke, tinged with a glimmer of hope. "Will she be all right, Doctor? What can we do to help her?"

Doctor Simmons offered a reassuring smile. "Rest, nourishment, and gentle care are key for her recovery. Ensure she remains in a calm environment. With time, she should regain consciousness."

Luke nodded, grateful for the doctor's guidance. "Thank you, Doctor. I will do everything I can to ensure her well-being."

Doctor Simmons placed a comforting hand on Luke's shoulder. "You have already shown great kindness and care. Now, be patient, and allow her body to heal."

As the doctor disappeared back into the bedroom, Luke stood outside, his thoughts consumed by a mixture of relief and concern. He understood the journey ahead would be one of patience and steadfast support.

With renewed determination, Luke prepared himself to provide the young woman with the care she needed, his heart buoyed by the hope that she would awaken and find solace under his roof.

As the moments stretched on, Luke found himself growing more anxious outside the bedroom door, his concern for the young woman deepening with every passing second. Finally, the door opened once again, and Doctor Simmons emerged with a look of relief etched upon his features.

"Luke, she has indeed suffered a concussion, as well as a few minor bruises, but I believe she will make a full recovery," the doctor informed him, his voice carrying a soothing tone. "With proper rest and care, she should regain consciousness in due time."

Relief flooded Luke's being, and a weight seemed to lift from his shoulders. A grateful smile crept across his face as he nodded in appreciation. "Thank you, Doctor

Simmons. Your expertise and reassurance mean a great deal to me."

The doctor returned the smile, his eyes filled with a mix of empathy and professional satisfaction. "It's my duty to assist those in need. I'm glad I could offer some comfort during this difficult time."

Luke's gaze shifted back to the woman lying in the room, his heart yearning to know more about her. Doctor Simmons followed his line of sight, a thoughtful expression on his face.

"Do you know who she is, Luke?" the doctor asked, curiosity evident in his voice. "Perhaps her name or any identifying information?"

Luke shook his head, a hint of disappointment tugging at him. "I'm afraid I don't. I found her being accosted by a sailor, and my priority was to ensure her safety. Until she awakens, it will be impossible to contact her family or determine her background."

The doctor nodded in understanding, his expression empathetic. "I see. Well, for now, our focus should be on her recovery. Once she regains consciousness, we can begin exploring her circumstances further."

Luke's mind buzzed with unanswered questions, but he knew the doctor's words held wisdom. He couldn't help but feel a sense of responsibility toward the young woman, a desire to ensure her well-being until her identity could be established.

With gratitude in his voice, Luke addressed the doctor. "Thank you for your guidance, Doctor Simmons. I will provide her with the care and support she needs. When she wakes, we can reassess the situation and determine the best course of action."

The doctor offered Luke a reassuring pat on the shoulder. "I have faith in your ability to provide her with the care she needs, Luke. Should any complications arise, don't hesitate to reach out. We will do our best to assist you."

As Doctor Simmons made his way toward the front door, ready to depart, Luke accompanied him, a mix of gratitude and determination evident in his eyes.

"Thank you again, Doctor. I'll ensure her recovery is my utmost priority," Luke expressed sincerely.

The doctor nodded, his voice filled with encouragement. "I have no doubt you will, Luke. Your compassion shines through in your actions. Take care of yourself as well."

With those parting words, the doctor bid farewell and departed, leaving Luke alone with his thoughts and the responsibility of caring for the young woman lying unconscious in his bedroom.

Taking a deep breath, Luke re-entered the room, his gaze filled with determination and a touch of apprehension. He knew the path ahead would not be easy, but he was resolved to provide the young woman with the same compassion and care he had shown to his own daughter.

As he stood by her side, he vowed to be her guardian until she regained consciousness, her presence now intertwining with his life in ways he couldn't yet fathom.

Chapter 10

Maggie woke with a start, her surroundings unfamiliar. The room was warmly lit, the fire crackling in the hearth. Her head throbbed with a dull pain, and she winced as she sat up. But the soft linen sheets that covered her were a far cry from the threadbare covers of her tenement bed, or the cold, unforgiving cobblestone street where she'd last been.

Standing by the fire was a little girl, her blonde curls tied up in ribbons. She wore a clean, pretty dress and was watching Maggie with wide eyes.

"Hello," Maggie greeted her, her voice hoarse.

"Hello," the girl replied. She seemed nervous, but also curiously excited. "You're awake. Papa said you might sleep all day, but I thought if I sat here and waited, you might wake up faster."

Maggie chuckled, the sound dry and a bit painful, but genuine. "That's kind of you. What's your name?"

"I'm Charlotte Axton. Papa brought you in after you… after you fell asleep." There was a careful pause, as if she was trying to choose her words. "He asked me not to disturb you. But I thought the company would help. Does it hurt a lot?"

Maggie touched her cheek, wincing at the tenderness. But she managed a reassuring smile. "I've had worse, little one. Thank you for your company."

They continued talking, Charlotte chattering away about her father, her dolls, and how she had watched Maggie sleep. Maggie listened, her eyes taking in the room. It was modest but warm, a world apart from the workhouse and the cold tenement rooms she was used to.

Maggie appreciated the company, and the distraction it provided from her own aching body and the unanswered questions that swirled in her mind. She thought of the boy with the warm brown eyes, of the sailor, of her brothers. She wasn't sure how she had ended up here, in this strange but comforting house, but she was grateful.

As she drifted back to sleep, cradled in the warmth of the Axton household and lulled by the sound of Charlotte's innocent chatter, she felt a glimmer of hope. Whatever tomorrow held, she would face it. For herself, for her brothers, and for the future they deserved.

The next time Maggie stirred, the fire had died down to embers, casting long shadows on the room's simple decor. She could hear the soft whistling of the wind outside, carrying with it the muffled sounds of a bustling city. Her body felt heavy and sluggish, but she could sense a marked improvement in her condition. Her head ached less, and the pain in her cheek had dulled to a mild throb.

A gentle knock sounded at the door, and a woman entered, carrying a tray of steaming broth and a cup of tea. She was an older woman, with soft, weathered features and a long braid of grey hair that fell over one shoulder. She wore a neat, dark dress and an apron, a clear sign of her position as a housekeeper.

"Good morning, dear," the woman greeted, her voice warm. "I'm Mrs Yates. I thought you might be awake. Can I help you sit up?"

Maggie nodded, gratefully accepting the woman's help as she propped up some pillows for support.

Just then, a small head peeked from behind the housekeeper. "Can I stay?" Charlotte asked, her eyes wide. "I promise I won't be a bother."

Mrs Yates looked momentarily flustered. "Charlotte, dear, the young lady needs her rest. Now off with you."

But Maggie intervened, surprising even herself. "No, it's all right. She can stay."

The housekeeper studied Maggie for a moment before relenting. "Very well, as long as you promise not to exhaust yourself. You need to rest."

Charlotte beamed, rushing to the side of the bed as Mrs Yates placed the tray on a small table next to the bed. The rich aroma of the chicken broth filled the room, making Maggie's stomach rumble with hunger.

"I thought some broth might be good to start with. Not too heavy," Mrs Yates said. She poured tea into a porcelain cup, placing it next to the bowl. "And some tea, to warm you up."

"Thank you, Mrs Yates," Maggie said, touched by the woman's kindness. She could not remember the last time someone had looked after her with such care.

Mrs Yates smiled, her eyes softening. "Just doing my job, dear. Now eat up, you need your strength."

With Charlotte's chatter filling the room and Mrs Yates' warm presence, Maggie felt something she hadn't felt in a very long time. A sense of home, of care, of being part of something. It was different from the bond she shared with Elaine and Dorothy, and she missed her brothers fiercely. Right here, though, she felt safe.

Spoonful by spoonful, Maggie started to eat the broth Mrs Yates had set before her. Despite the worries that churned inside her, she couldn't deny her hunger, or the comforting aroma of the home-cooked meal. As she ate, she took in her surroundings; the room was clean and orderly, with a soft warmth radiating from the hearth.

Little Charlotte remained by the fire, her eyes wide and curious as she watched Maggie. The silence between them was comfortable, not tense, and for that, Maggie was grateful. The little girl was a welcome distraction from the storm of thoughts whirling inside her head.

"Maggie?" Charlotte broke the silence, her voice small. "Did it hurt when you fell?"

Maggie looked at her, her spoon halfway to her mouth. "Yes," she admitted, with a grimace. "It did. I'm feeling better now."

Charlotte's eyes widened even further. "You're brave," she said, her voice carrying a clear note of admiration.

Maggie smiled, although the compliment made her heart ache. She was no hero; she was a sister desperate to find her brothers.

Mrs Yates sat down on a stool next to the bed, her hands folded in her lap. "As we said before, Mr Axton found you on the street. He carried you back here, and we've been looking after you ever since."

"And the man who attacked me?" Maggie asked, her voice barely more than a whisper.

Mrs Yates sighed, her expression grave. "Mr Axton dealt with him, dear. Don't worry yourself about that."

Maggie nodded, a rush of relief washing over her. She was safe, at least for now, and for that, she was profoundly grateful. She glanced over at Charlotte, whose wide eyes were still fixed on her. Maggie mustered a smile for the girl.

"Thank you," she said to them both. "For everything."

"Doctor Simmons came while you were unconscious," Mrs Yates began, smoothing her apron in her lap, "He's a good man, the town's physician. He said you'd been through a rough ordeal, but he reckons with enough rest, you'll recover soon enough."

Maggie listened to her words, a small spark of gratitude flickering within her. It was a minor consolation in the grand scheme of things, but it was something. A lifeline in the storm she found herself in.

"What about...?" She started to ask, her voice faltering as she thought of the sailor. She was not keen to revisit the memory, but she needed to know.

"Mr Axton ensured that the man wouldn't bother you again," Mrs Yates reassured her gently, catching her meaning without her having to spell it out. "He... can be very persuasive when he needs to be."

"I can't thank him, or you, enough," Maggie said, her voice soft with sincerity. "You didn't have to take me in. You didn't even know me."

Mrs Yates offered her a warm smile, one that held a motherly fondness. "There's a saying around here, dear," she said, "In our town, we look after each other. That's just how things work around here."

Maggie looked down, her heart filling with a painful mix of relief and guilt. She was being cared for by strangers while her brothers were... where? The question hung in the air, a cruel echo that followed her every thought.

Charlotte, sensing the tension in the room, piped up from her corner by the fire. "Do you have a favourite colour, Maggie?"

The question startled Maggie. It was so innocent, so simple, that it broke the cloud of heavy thoughts hanging around her.

"I..." she started, then laughed softly. "Yes, I suppose I do. It's blue."

"Like the sky?" Charlotte asked, her eyes lighting up.

Maggie nodded, smiling despite herself. "Exactly, like the sky."

Mrs Yates offered a gentle smile, before standing. "I should inform Mr Axton that you're awake, dear," she said softly, "he'll want to know you are awake."

"No need to rush, Mrs Yates," Maggie insisted as the older woman stood, concern lining her features. "I'm perfectly fine."

The housekeeper cast a glance in her direction, something unreadable flickering in her eyes. "I know, dear. But Mr Axton was quite worried when he brought you in. He hardly left your side until I managed to convince him that he was needed elsewhere. He'd want to know that you're awake and well."

Maggie nodded, understanding. From what Mrs Yates and Charlotte had shared, this Mr Axton had done much to ensure her safety. A pang of gratitude washed over her. She had not had many instances in her life to feel such a sentiment. But as she sat in the comfort of the room, safe and cared for, it felt like the most natural feeling in the world.

A soft knock echoed in the room before Mrs Yates departed, leaving Maggie alone with Charlotte. The young girl looked up from her play, her bright eyes filled with curiosity.

"Is it true, what they say about sailors?" she asked, her tone hushed as if they were sharing secrets. "That they're rough and ruthless?"

Maggie offered a small smile, her heart aching with the harsh reality of the world she had come to know. "Some of them are, Charlotte," she admitted softly. "But some are also kind and gentle. The world isn't just black and white, you see."

Before Charlotte could respond, the door creaked open, revealing the silhouette of a man. Charlotte's face instantly lit up. "Papa!" she exclaimed, rushing to him.

Mr Axton - for that's who he had to be - was a tall man, with warm brown eyes that mirrored his daughter's. His features were kind, a stark contrast to the harshness Maggie had come to expect from the world. He scooped Charlotte up in his arms, balancing her on his hip as he approached Maggie's bedside.

"Miss Barlow," he greeted, his voice as gentle as his demeanour. "I'm glad to see you awake."

The sincerity in his eyes, the kindness in his voice, it was all too much. Tears pricked at the corners of Maggie's eyes as she offered him a small nod. "Thank you, Mr Axton. For everything."

He just smiled, a soft, understanding curve of his lips. "You're most welcome, Miss Barlow."

For the first time in a long while, Maggie felt a sense of safety, a flicker of hope. And in that moment, she vowed to herself that she would find her brothers, that she would provide for them the same safety she had been granted by these kind strangers.

Chapter 11

Luke's heart skipped a beat as he entered the room and saw the young woman, Maggie, awake and wearing a gentle smile. Relief washed over him, and he approached her bedside with a mixture of caution and joy.

"Maggie," he greeted, his voice filled with a blend of relief and warmth. "I'm glad to see you awake. How are you feeling?"

Maggie's eyes sparkled with a light that belied the hardships she had endured. Her smile, radiant and genuine, seemed to illuminate the room. "I feel much better now, thank you. It's kind of you to take care of me."

Luke's concern melted away, replaced by a sense of awe at Maggie's resilience. He found himself captivated by her spirit, her ability to maintain cheerfulness despite the events of the previous night.

"You're most welcome, Maggie," Luke replied, his voice tender and earnest. "I couldn't stand by and let any harm come to you. You're safe now."

Maggie's expression turned curious as she observed her surroundings, her gaze landing on Luke. "Can you tell me what happened? I remember bits and pieces, but it's all a bit blurry."

Luke took a deep breath, searching for the right words to explain the events without causing her distress. He wanted to shield her from the memories of the assault and focus on her recovery and well-being.

"There was an altercation with a drunken sailor," Luke began, choosing his words carefully. "I happened to be passing by and intervened. You were struck and lost consciousness. Now, you're in a safe place, and there's no need to worry."

Maggie's eyes narrowed in thought, her brow furrowing slightly as she tried to recall the details. "I see... Thank you for helping me, Mr Axton. You've been so kind."

Luke's heart swelled at her gratitude, appreciating the sincerity in her voice. He wanted nothing more than to provide her comfort and support during her recovery.

"You're welcome, Maggie," he responded, his voice laced with warmth. "I'm just glad I could be there for you. You're a strong and resilient young woman. And please, call me Luke."

Maggie's smile brightened, filling the room with an air of hope and gratitude. "You've shown me such kindness, Luke. I don't know how to repay you."

Luke waved off her gratitude, his own smile mirroring hers. "There's no need for repayment, Maggie. Knowing that you're safe and on the path to recovery is more than enough for me."

They sat in companionable silence for a moment, the weight of unspoken words lingering in the air. Luke found solace in Maggie's presence, a reminder of the strength of the human spirit even in the face of adversity.

As the seconds ticked by, Luke realised that their lives had intersected in an unexpected way, and he was determined to provide Maggie with the care and support she deserved.

As Luke listened to Maggie's explanation, a mix of concern and determination settled within him. He understood the importance of her work and the responsibilities she held, but he couldn't bear the thought of her returning to the very place where she had been attacked so soon.

"Maggie," he began, his voice gentle yet firm, "I understand your dedication to your work, but your well-being is paramount. You need time to recover fully before returning to that environment."

Maggie's brows furrowed in contemplation, her eyes meeting Luke's with a mix of gratitude and uncertainty. "I appreciate your concern, Luke, but I can't afford to miss work. It's how I make a living."

Luke's expression softened as he reached out, placing a hand on Maggie's shoulder. "I understand the importance of work, but your health and safety are equally important. Please, allow me to help you during this time. You can stay here until you're fully recovered and ready to face the challenges ahead."

Maggie's gaze wavered, torn between the necessity of work and the genuine care Luke had shown her. She sighed softly, her voice filled with a hint of vulnerability. "I don't want to burden you, Luke. You've already done so much for me."

Luke smiled reassuringly, his grip on her shoulder tightening slightly. "You're not a burden, Maggie. I have the means and the desire to help you. It would be my honour to provide you with a safe place to recover. We can work together to find a solution that allows you to take the time you need without jeopardising your livelihood."

Maggie's eyes flickered with a mix of gratitude and relief, her shoulders visibly relaxing under Luke's touch. She nodded slowly, her voice filled with a newfound trust. "Thank you, Luke. Your kindness overwhelms me. I'll accept your offer and stay until I'm fully healed."

Luke's smile widened, grateful for her acceptance. He knew that providing her with a safe haven during her recovery was the right decision. He was determined to be there for her, just as he had been during that fateful encounter.

"Thank you," he replied, his voice carrying a blend of gratitude and reassurance. "Together, we'll ensure your well-being and find a way to address your work situation. You're not alone in this."

In that moment, Luke's determination to protect and care for Maggie grew stronger. He would do everything in his power to provide her with the support she needed, both physically and emotionally.

With a shared understanding, they settled into a comfortable silence, ready to face the obstacles that awaited them.

Chapter 12

The soft morning light filtered through the windows of Luke's humble abode, casting a warm glow on the room. Luke had just finished preparing breakfast when a knock at the door startled him. Surprised, he hurried to answer it, only to find Esther standing on the threshold, her face a mixture of surprise and displeasure.

"Esther," Luke exclaimed, his voice filled with a mix of surprise and concern. "What brings you here so early in the morning?"

Esther's eyes darted around the room, landing on Maggie, who sat quietly in the corner. Anger flared in Esther's gaze, her voice laced with accusation. "Luke, who is she? Why is she here?"

Luke's brow furrowed as he stepped aside, motioning for Esther to enter. "Please, come in, Esther. Let's talk."

Esther hesitated for a moment before stepping inside, her gaze fixed firmly on Maggie. "I demand an explanation, Luke. Why is this woman in our home?"

Luke led Esther to a chair, his voice calm yet pleading. "Her name is Maggie. She was attacked last night, and I found her in need of help. I couldn't just leave her, Esther. She needed a safe place to recover."

Esther's eyes widened, a mix of disbelief and anger flashing across her features. "Attacked? And you brought her here? What were you thinking? This is unacceptable!"

Luke's tone remained steady, his voice filled with conviction. "Esther, please try to understand. Maggie was in danger, and I couldn't turn my back on her. I simply asked her to stay until she's fully recovered."

Esther's frustration mounted, her voice rising with each word. "Luke, how can you prioritise a stranger over me? We have a life together, a future! This woman means nothing to you!"

Luke's heart sank as he realised the depth of Esther's anger and hurt. He reached out, attempting to bridge the gap between them. "Esther, you mean the world to me. But compassion and kindness should not be limited. I wanted to help someone in need, and I can't apologise for that."

Esther's gaze wavered, her emotions in turmoil. "I won't have another woman in your home."

Luke's voice softened, his eyes pleading for understanding. "Esther, I know this is difficult, but Maggie needs my support right now. I promise, once she's recovered, she will leave, and we can resume our plans together."

Esther's anger seemed to subside, replaced by a mix of hurt and resignation. She sighed deeply, her voice laden with sadness. "Luke, I don't know if I can accept this. It feels like our foundation has been shaken."

Luke's heart ached at Esther's words, the weight of the situation pressing upon him. He took a step closer, reaching out to touch her arm gently. "Esther, please give me the chance to make things right. I care for you, but in this moment, I cannot turn my back on someone in need."

Esther's gaze hardened, her voice tinged with frustration. "I can't believe you're choosing her over me, Luke. I can't stand to be around someone who puts strangers before me."

Luke's patience waned, his own anger rising to the surface. "Esther, it's not about choosing anyone over you. It's about showing compassion and humanity to someone in need. I expected more understanding from you."

Esther's face contorted with a mix of hurt and indignation. "You don't understand, Luke! You don't understand how it feels to be replaced, to feel second best!"

Luke's voice grew sharper as his anger ignited. "This has nothing to do with being replaced! I asked for your support and understanding, and instead, you're making it about yourself. This is not the way to act in front of Maggie, or around Charlotte."

The tension in the room became palpable, the air thick with unspoken words and shattered expectations. Esther, her pride wounded, stormed towards the door, her voice dripping with anger and hurt. "I can't be here, Luke. Not with her around. Figure out what's more important to you."

With those words, Esther slammed the door shut behind her, leaving Luke standing alone in the silence of his home. His chest heaved with a mix of frustration and sadness, the weight of the situation pressing heavily upon him.

Luke's gaze flickered to Maggie, who sat quietly, witnessing the heated exchange. He sighed deeply, realising the impact their argument had on her as well. With a heavy heart, he approached Maggie, his voice filled with genuine concern. "I'm sorry you had to witness that, Maggie. It's not how I wanted things to unfold."

Maggie's eyes met his, her expression filled with empathy. "Luke, don't worry about me. I understand the complexities of the situation. You did what you believed was right, and that's commendable."

Luke nodded, gratitude swelling within him for Maggie's understanding. "Thank you, Maggie. Your support means a great deal to me."

In the wake of Esther's departure, the air seemed to hold a mix of tension and uncertainty. Luke knew that he would need to navigate the aftermath of their argument and focus on supporting Maggie during her recovery.

With a resolute determination, Luke vowed to stay true to his principles, embracing the responsibility he had taken upon himself. He couldn't deny the turmoil in his heart, but he knew that helping someone in need was the right path, regardless of the challenges it brought.

Chapter 13

"Luke," Maggie began, the morning sunlight streaming in through the dining room window. "I cannot impose on you any further, especially after what happened with Esther earlier. I appreciate all that you've done, but I must return to work."

Luke Axton sat across the table, his steaming cup of tea poised in his hand. Charlotte sat between them, happily scooping up mouthfuls of porridge with chunks of apples baked into it, a far cry from the meagre meals Maggie was used to. The delicious smell of toasted bread and cured ham, a side dish to their main meal, wafted up from the plate, making her stomach rumble despite her worries.

"Nonsense," Luke waved off her protests, his gentle eyes steady on hers. "You've had a fright, Maggie. You need rest. Let me speak to your employer, explain the situation."

"But—" she began to protest, but he raised a hand to halt her.

"Please," he implored, his gaze softening. "It's the least I can do."

The sincerity in his voice was hard to ignore. It was also hard to overlook how her heart fluttered at the notion of someone looking out for her, a sensation alien to her. The thick lump in her throat was testament to the gratitude she felt, yet couldn't voice. She swallowed it down, managing to nod at him. "Thank you, Mr Axton."

He smiled at her warmly, lifting his cup in a silent toast before taking a sip.

"And I'll keep you company while Papa is gone!" Charlotte chirped in suddenly, a spoonful of porridge suspended midway to her mouth, her wide eyes sparkling with excitement. "We can play dolls!"

Maggie laughed softly at the girl's enthusiasm, her heart aching in a bitter-sweet way. Oh, how she wished her brothers could have had such a childhood, filled with warmth and carefree joy.

She cast a look at Mr Axton, whose eyes mirrored the same gentleness his daughter's held. For a moment, the heaviness in her heart lightened. A fleeting thought crossed her mind that maybe, just maybe, not all was lost.

As Luke Axton headed out the door, Maggie stood, refusing to sit idle while Mrs Yates cleaned up after breakfast. "Please, Mrs Yates," she pleaded with the housekeeper. "I can help clean up."

With a sigh, Mrs Yates relented, handing her a cloth and nodding towards the soiled dishes. Maggie set to work, scrubbing the remnants of their breakfast away with measured, rhythmic strokes. The humdrum activity had always had a soothing effect on her, providing a backdrop for her thoughts to settle against.

Charlotte was by her side in an instant, her small hands reaching for a dish, mimicking Maggie's movements. It was then that Maggie was struck with how mature Charlotte seemed for her age, doing chores without complaint, her eagerness to help unquestionable. "You're a good girl, Charlotte," Maggie remarked, a warm smile tugging at her lips.

Charlotte beamed up at her, her innocent eyes sparkling. "Mama taught me well before she passed away," she admitted with a touch of melancholy tinging her voice. The simple mention of her mother's death hung in the air, heavy and ominous, the cheerful morning sunlight doing little to lift the sudden gloom.

A pang of sympathy pierced Maggie's heart. She had known the sting of loss all too well, the hole it left behind in one's life all too vast to fill. "I'm sorry to hear about your mother, Charlotte," she murmured, laying a hand on the little girl's shoulder. "She must have been a wonderful woman to have raised such a good daughter."

Charlotte nodded, her gaze downcast. "It was two years ago," she confessed, her voice barely above a whisper. "I still miss her every day."

"Two years," Maggie echoed, her own mother's abandonment surfacing in her mind. She could not fathom how Charlotte felt, having had a mother who cared, only to be taken away so suddenly. All she could offer was a sympathetic ear and a shared understanding of life's cruelties.

"I'm sure she's proud of you, wherever she is," Maggie reassured, giving Charlotte's shoulder a gentle squeeze. Her words hung in the air, a beacon of comfort amidst their shared losses. Perhaps, she mused, they were not so different after all, both having been shaped by the loss of a mother, albeit in starkly different ways.

As they continued with their chores in shared silence, a newfound bond began to take root between them, stemming from their mutual understanding of grief, and the shared yearning for what they had lost.

***

Luke returned later that morning, his face flushed from the brisk walk, his eyes shining with satisfaction. As he entered, Maggie was still washing the last of the dishes. When she saw him, her heart skipped a beat. She hastily dried her hands and turned to him.

"I convinced Mrs Smith to grant you some time off," Luke began, his tone casual as he removed his coat and hat. "She's not happy about it, but I promised to order several dresses for Charlotte. It seemed a fair exchange."

Relief flooded Maggie. She had been dreading the prospect of having to return to work in her current state. While she had begun to regain some strength, the incident had left her shaky and drained. The prospect of sewing delicate stitches in the rich fabrics that Mrs Smith preferred felt overwhelming.

"Thank you, Luke," she said, her gratitude pouring out in her words. "You've been so kind. I don't know how I'll ever repay you."

Luke waved off her gratitude with a good-natured smile, his eyes soft. "There's no need for that, Maggie. We look out for each other, right?"

There was something about the warmth in his gaze, the gentle slope of his smile, that made her heart flutter. She found herself blushing, a wave of unfamiliar emotions washing over her. Was this gratitude she was feeling? Or was it something more?

Suddenly, she was aware of the way his brown eyes sparkled, the way his hair was tousled in just the right way, the broadness of his shoulders. There was an undeniable kindness in him, a strength and protectiveness that drew her in.

She wasn't quite sure when she had begun noticing these details about him. Perhaps it was when he had first carried her into his home, or when he had comforted her in her fears. But now, she saw him in a new light. She saw not just a saviour, but a man she could imagine herself with, a man she found herself falling for.

However, she pushed those thoughts aside, reminding herself of her circumstances. She was still in recovery, still in search of her brothers, still uncertain about her future. She had to focus on her immediate problems before considering the longings of her heart.

But as Luke made his way towards the kitchen to pour himself a cup of tea, chatting away about his conversation with Mrs Smith, Maggie couldn't help but feel a warm sensation in her chest. And though she was unsure of what the future might hold, she was certain of one thing - for the first time in a long time, she was not alone. And that thought brought her more comfort than any blanket ever could.

Chapter 14

The sun was streaming through the window when Maggie woke. She blinked, rubbing the sleep from her eyes, then sat up, startled to find Charlotte by her bedside, holding a tray laden with a simple but hearty breakfast.

"I didn't mean to wake you," Charlotte said with a bashful smile. "Papa told me to bring you some breakfast. He said you shouldn't exert yourself yet."

Maggie felt a pang of gratitude for Luke's thoughtful gesture. "That's kind of you, Charlotte. Thank you." She accepted the tray from the little girl, admiring the perfectly browned toast, the neatly cut wedges of cheese, the fresh strawberries, and the steamy mug of tea. A luxuriously comforting meal compared to the meagre rations she was used to.

As Maggie started to eat, Charlotte settled herself by her bedside, her eyes wide with curiosity. "Do you like being a seamstress?" she asked, a question that clearly had been bubbling in her mind.

Maggie paused, considering the question. She had never thought of her work as something to be loved or hated. It was a necessity, a means to an end. But as she thought about it, she found herself smiling.

"Yes, I suppose I do," she admitted. "There's a sense of accomplishment in taking a piece of fabric and transforming it into something beautiful and useful. It's rewarding when a dress fits just right, or when a customer is pleased with the alterations. I was never good with a needle, until I started work there - strangely, it was my brothers who were good at tailoring. Although I don't think there will be much use for it in a factory."

Her mind drifted back to the countless hours she had spent in Mrs Smith's shop, hunched over the sewing machine, her fingers deftly manoeuvring the needle and thread. Each stitch was a testament to her patience and skill, each garment a reflection of her artistry. Despite the gruelling hours and the demanding clientele, there was an undeniable satisfaction in her work.

Charlotte listened attentively, her eyes bright with interest. "It sounds wonderful," she breathed. "Can you teach me how to sew one day?"

Maggie laughed, the sound filling the quiet room. "Of course, Charlotte. When I'm feeling better, I'll show you how to sew a basic stitch. We'll start with a handkerchief, how does that sound?"

Charlotte nodded eagerly, her face lighting up. "I can't wait, Maggie!"

And as they chatted away the morning, with Charlotte hanging on to her every word and laughing at her small jokes, Maggie found herself thinking that maybe, just maybe, she could find a place for herself in this new world, in this home filled with warmth, kindness, and the promise of a brighter future.

Maggie put down the empty plate, her stomach satisfyingly full. The mood in the room shifted, the early morning sunlight softening the edges of their conversation. Charlotte, her tiny face earnest, broke the silence.

"You talked about your brothers earlier," Charlotte said. "What happened to them?"

Maggie sighed, looking down at her hands. "We were separated when I was sent to work for the seamstress. They were sent to a factory to work, but I don't know where. I've been trying to find them ever since."

"Oh," Charlotte breathed, her brows furrowed in thought. "That's so sad."

"Yes," Maggie agreed, her heart aching with the memory of her brothers' smiles. "But I'm not giving up. I'll find them someday."

Charlotte reached out to squeeze Maggie's hand, a tiny, comforting gesture that meant more than any words could. "I hope you do. I would love to meet them."

The air around them seemed to shimmer with shared sorrow, the invisible threads of their lives woven together in that moment. They were both marked by loss, shaped by the absence of loved ones. But there was also resilience, a quiet determination to keep moving forward, to never give up.

"I think you would get along with William," Maggie said, a small smile playing on her lips as she thought of her brother. "He's got this infectious laugh, and he's always up to something."

Charlotte giggled. "He sounds like a handful."

"He is," Maggie admitted with a chuckle. "But he's also sweet and caring. You'd love him."

Their conversation drifted on, moving from heartache to hope, weaving a bond of shared experiences and dreams. They talked of their past and their hopes for the future. They shared stories of their loved ones, painting vivid pictures with their words, keeping their memories alive.

By the time they finished, the room was bathed in the golden light of the late morning sun. Maggie felt a sense of peace she hadn't experienced in a long time, comforted by the companionship of a little girl who understood her pain and shared her hopes.

"I hope you find your brothers, Maggie," Charlotte said earnestly. "I really do."

"And I hope you never have to know the pain of losing a sibling," Maggie responded, squeezing Charlotte's hand.

With a mutual nod of understanding, they let the silence settle around them, their shared companionship creating a comfort against the world outside the door. It was a balm against the harsh realities of their past and the uncertainty of the future, a promise of solace in the days to come. And for now, that was enough.

Chapter 15

Luke walked past the bedroom door, his thoughts still consumed by the recent upheaval. However, as he passed by, a familiar sound caught his attention—a soft, melodic laughter. Luke's steps faltered, and he leaned closer, straining to hear the conversation inside.

Inside the room, he found Maggie and Charlotte engaged in lively chatter, their voices filled with joy and warmth. Charlotte's laughter, so rare since her mother's passing, filled the air like a gentle breeze, soothing Luke's troubled heart.

A bittersweet smile tugged at Luke's lips as he listened to their interaction. He couldn't deny the genuine connection between Maggie and his daughter, how effortlessly they seemed to bond. It warmed his heart to see Charlotte finding joy and laughter in the presence of someone new.

Luke leaned against the doorframe, his heart swelling with a mix of gratitude and appreciation. He observed the way Maggie's eyes sparkled with genuine interest and care as she engaged with Charlotte, the way her laughter mingled harmoniously with his daughter's.

In that moment, a realisation settled within Luke—a growing fondness and affection for Maggie. Her presence had become a comforting presence in their home, filling the void left by his late wife. He admired her strength, her resilience, and the genuine kindness she exuded.

As he stood there, witnessing the blossoming connection between Maggie and Charlotte, Luke found himself envisioning a future where they formed a united family—a family forged from shared experiences, support, and love.

But in the midst of his budding feelings, Luke couldn't help but acknowledge the complexities of the situation. He was still nursing the wounds from his recent argument with Esther, and the timing felt uncertain.

Yet, in the serenity of that moment, with Charlotte's laughter dancing in his ears, Luke made a silent vow—to continue nurturing the bond between Maggie and his daughter, and to explore the growing connection he felt with Maggie himself, all while remaining sensitive to the emotions and needs of everyone involved.

Taking a deep breath, he mustered the strength to move away from the doorframe, knowing that their path forward would require patience, understanding, and open communication.

With renewed determination, Luke pushed open the door, his heart brimming with affection. He entered the room, his voice filled with warmth. "What's all this laughter about? Am I missing out on the fun?"

Charlotte's eyes widened in delight as she saw her father enter, and Maggie's smile grew wider, reaching her eyes. "Oh, Daddy! You should've heard the funny story Maggie just told. She's so good at making me laugh!"

Luke's own smile blossomed as he approached them, the connection between them palpable. "Is that so? Well, I'm glad to see both of you enjoying each other's company. Laughter is a precious gift."

As they shared the moment, Luke couldn't help but wonder what the future held for their unconventional family. But for now, he focused on fostering the bond between them, cherishing the joy and laughter that filled their home, and allowing his feelings for Maggie to grow, knowing that love had a way of finding its own path in due time.

Luke turned to leave the room, content with the harmony he had witnessed between Charlotte and Maggie. However, as he reached for the doorknob, he felt a gentle touch on his arm. He turned back to see

Maggie looking up at him, a glimmer of hope in her eyes.

"Luke, would you mind staying a little longer?" Maggie asked, her voice filled with a mix of vulnerability and determination. "I feel comfortable talking with you, and there's something else I'd like to share."

Luke's surprise gave way to a surge of happiness. To be included in such a vulnerable moment was a testament to the trust they were building. He nodded eagerly, a gentle smile playing on his lips. "Of course, Maggie. I'll stay as long as you need."

Maggie's eyes softened with gratitude, and she gestured for him to take a seat. As they settled, Maggie's gaze became distant, her voice tinged with longing. "We were talking about family, Luke. I have two brothers, William and Thomas, and I've been searching for them for a long time."

Luke listened intently, his heart swelling with empathy for Maggie's longing to reunite with her family. He could see the profound value she placed on family bonds, and it resonated deeply within him.

Maggie continued, her voice carrying a mix of hope and uncertainty. "We were separated when we were young, and it has been a constant ache in my heart not knowing where they are or if they're safe. I've been trying to find them, and I won't give up until I do."

Luke reached out and placed a hand on Maggie's, offering comfort and support. "Maggie, your determination and love for your family are truly admirable. I hope with all my heart that you find your brothers and that your family can be reunited."

Maggie's eyes welled with emotion, her voice quivering with gratitude. "Thank you, Luke. Your encouragement means more than you know. I believe that someday, with enough perseverance, we will find each other again."

In that moment, Luke's admiration for Maggie deepened. Her resilience, her unwavering love for her family, and her ability to find hope amidst the uncertainties of life stirred his own emotions. He felt himself falling even harder for her, drawn to her strength and the values they shared.

Luke's mind drifted to thoughts of Esther as he observed the genuine affection between Maggie and Charlotte. A pang of realisation coursed through him as he compared Maggie's unwavering adoration for his daughter to the strained relationship between Charlotte and Esther.

He couldn't help but wonder if Esther had only shown kindness to Charlotte when he was around, putting on a facade that crumbled once he was out of sight. The realisation hit him with a tinge of regret, as he questioned his own perception and the depth of their connection.

Deep down, Luke had hoped that Esther would embrace Charlotte as her own, but the reality of their strained relationship now seemed undeniable. He pondered whether he had been too blinded by his own desire for a stable family unit to recognise the truth.

Maggie noticed the shift in Luke's demeanour and her concern grew. She gently placed a hand on his arm, her voice filled with empathy. "Luke, you seem lost in thought. Is something troubling you?"

Luke sighed softly, appreciating Maggie's kindness and understanding. He met her gaze and decided to share his concerns, albeit cautiously. "I can't help but notice how easily Charlotte connects with you, Maggie. It's such a stark contrast to her relationship with Esther. I wonder if I've been blind to the truth, if Esther's kindness to Charlotte was only when I was around."

Maggie's expression softened, her eyes reflecting understanding. She removed her hand from Luke's arm but kept her gaze locked with his. "Luke, sometimes it takes time to see the true nature of a person's relationships. It's possible that Esther may have struggled to connect with Charlotte genuinely, and you might not have noticed it at first."

Luke nodded, grateful for Maggie's insights and validation. "You're right, Maggie. I wanted so desperately for Esther to embrace Charlotte, to create a loving family. Maybe I overlooked the signs though, hoping for a different outcome."

Maggie reached out, placing a comforting hand on Luke's arm. "It's natural to want a stable and loving family unit, Luke. But what matters most is Charlotte's well-being and happiness."

Luke's gratitude welled within him, his voice filled with sincerity. "Thank you,

Maggie. Your understanding and support mean more than you know. I'm grateful to have you by our side."

Maggie offered him a warm smile, her compassion evident. "After all you've done, some well-meaning advice is the least I can do."

Luke gently nudged Charlotte then, remembering why he was here. "Charlotte, my dear, could you please tidy up for dinner? We'll be eating together tonight."

Charlotte looked up from her conversation with Maggie, her eyes brightening at the prospect of a shared meal. "Of course, Papa!"

Luke's heart swelled with love and pride as he watched his daughter take responsibility with such eagerness. He turned to Maggie, a hopeful smile playing on his lips. "Maggie, would you join us for dinner tonight? It would mean a great deal to have you at the table with us."

Maggie's eyes shimmered with gratitude and a touch of excitement. "I would be honoured, Luke. Thank you for including me."

Luke led the way to the dining room, Charlotte trailing behind, humming a tune as she tidied up. He pulled out a chair for Maggie, his eyes meeting hers with a mix of tenderness and anticipation.

As they gathered around the table, the air filled with a sense of togetherness and the promise of a shared meal. Luke couldn't help but feel a profound sense of gratitude for the company he had found in Maggie and the newfound hope that had blossomed within their home.

As they enjoyed the meal, laughter and conversation filled the room, intermingled with the clinking of cutlery and the warmth of shared stories. Luke looked at Maggie and Charlotte, their faces illuminated by the flickering candlelight, and his heart swelled with a sense of belonging.

At that moment, he couldn't help but think about the upcoming day. The demands of his job at the warehouse weighed heavily on his mind, yet he found solace in the knowledge that he had found a support system in Maggie and the love he held for Charlotte.

As the evening came to a close, Luke rose from his seat, a sense of gratitude radiating from him. "Thank you, Maggie, for joining us tonight. Your presence brought a special warmth to our family dinner."

Maggie's smile was genuine, her eyes reflecting the bond that had formed between them. "It was my pleasure, Luke. Your family has welcomed me with open arms, and I'm grateful for the connection we share."

Luke walked Maggie to the door, his hand brushing against hers in a gentle gesture of appreciation. "Tomorrow, I must return to work, but I'll be thinking of you and Charlotte. Please know that you have a place in our lives."

Maggie's eyes met Luke's, a touch of longing and understanding present. "Thank you, Luke. Your kindness and acceptance mean the world to me. Take care tomorrow, and I'll eagerly await your return."

Luke tenderly tucked Charlotte into bed, his touch filled with affection and warmth. He leaned over to place a gentle kiss on her forehead, his voice soft and soothing. "Goodnight, my dear Charlotte. Sleep well."

As Charlotte nestled into her pillows, a quiet sigh escaped her lips. Luke sat on the edge of the bed, his gaze fixed on his daughter's face, his heart swelling with both joy and melancholy. "What's on your mind, my sweet Charlotte?"

Charlotte turned to face her father, her eyes glistening with unshed tears. "I'm happy, Papa. I'm happy that Maggie is here with us. She's kind and funny, and I'll be really sad when she has to leave."

Luke's heart ached with understanding, his own emotions mirroring his daughter's. He reached out to wipe away a tear that had escaped Charlotte's eye, his voice filled with tenderness. "I know, my love. Maggie has brought so much joy and love into our lives. I'll be sad to see her leave too."

Charlotte sniffled, her voice wavering with genuine emotion. "Do you think... do you think she'll come back, Papa? Will we see her again?"

Luke's gaze softened, his heart yearning for the answer his daughter sought. "I can't say for certain, my dear. But I believe that the connections we forge with people are not easily broken. If it's meant to be, I have faith that our paths will cross again."

Charlotte nodded, finding solace in her father's words. She clutched her favourite stuffed animal tightly, seeking comfort in its familiar presence. "I'll miss her, but I'm grateful for the time we've had together."

Luke smiled lovingly, his hand gently stroking Charlotte's hair. "And I am grateful too, my sweet Charlotte. We were blessed to have Maggie in our lives, even if it's only for a little while. Let's cherish the memories we've made together."

With a final kiss on her forehead, Luke bid Charlotte goodnight, leaving her to the embrace of sleep. As he walked away from her room, he couldn't shake the heaviness in his heart, knowing that their time with Maggie was indeed limited.

In the quiet solitude of his own room, Luke allowed himself to feel the depth of his emotions. He had developed strong feelings for Maggie, feelings that extended beyond mere friendship. The thought of her leaving weighed heavily on him, and he longed for the possibility of a future together.

Yet, in the midst of his longing, Luke recognised the importance of embracing the present and cherishing the moments they had shared. He knew that life's circumstances sometimes took people away from us, but the impact they made on our hearts remained.

With a determined resolve, Luke whispered into the silence of the room, his voice filled with conviction. "I will cherish the time we have left, and I will keep the hope alive in my heart. Whatever the future holds, the connection we share with Maggie will forever be a cherished part of our lives."

Chapter 16

Maggie gathered her cloak and bag, her heart heavy. The room was cosy and filled with warm light from the hearth, making the prospect of stepping out into the cold morning even harder. Luke and Charlotte stood nearby, their expressions a mix of sadness and understanding.

"Maggie," Luke began, his voice gentle but persistent, "you don't have to go. We have room here."

"I can't impose on you any longer, Luke," Maggie replied, her gaze steady. She appreciated his offer, his kindness, but she couldn't accept it. Not when she had a responsibility to Mrs Smith. Not when she had the prospect of finding her brothers to consider.

"You're not imposing," Charlotte piped up, her small voice echoing in the quiet room. "We like having you here."

A warm, tender smile spread across Maggie's face. "I liked being here too, Charlotte. Very much. But Mrs Smith expects me back. I've already overstayed."

"Then we'll speak with her. We can explain," Luke said, stepping forward.

Maggie shook her head. "It's not just about the job, Luke." She hesitated, meeting his gaze. "I need to find my brothers. I can't stop searching for them."

Luke nodded, understanding washing over his features. "I... I can't say I understand how you're feeling, but I respect your decision."

Maggie stepped forward, placing a hand on Luke's arm. "Thank you, Luke. For understanding."

"And we can help," Charlotte added, looking at her Papa with pleading eyes. "We can help find your brothers, right, Papa?"

Luke looked at his daughter, then back at Maggie. After a moment, he nodded. "Yes. If Maggie needs us to help her, of course we will, Charlotte love."

A rush of gratitude flooded through Maggie. She knew she was making the right decision leaving, but it warmed her heart knowing that she was leaving friends behind.

"Thank you, but I can't stay here forever" she responded, voice choked with emotion.

Luke gave her a kind, sad smile. "I know."

Overwhelmed, Maggie nodded. "Thank you, Luke. Thank you, Charlotte."

In the end, she walked out into the cold morning, a bittersweet ache in her heart. But she also left with the comforting knowledge that she wasn't alone in her quest, that she had friends in this harsh world, willing to stand by her. She took one last look at the cosy room, etching the memory in her heart, before stepping out into the world once again.

Upon reaching the tenement building, Maggie was greeted by two worried faces.

Elaine and Dorothy, their eyes filled with relief upon seeing her.

"Maggie!" Dorothy exclaimed, rushing forward to engulf Maggie in a tight hug. "We've been worried sick. Where have you been?"

"I'm so sorry," Maggie said, her voice muffled in the folds of Dorothy's dress. "I didn't mean to worry you."

"We thought something had happened to you," Elaine added, her brows furrowed with worry.

Maggie pulled back from Dorothy and nodded at Elaine. "Something did happen," she began. "But I'm all right now."

The story flowed from Maggie's lips, but each word felt like a betrayal to the warmth and comfort she had left behind. She spoke of the drunken sailor, the unconsciousness that had followed, and then waking up in the home of the man who saved her.

"And his name is Luke?" Dorothy asked, once Maggie had finished her tale.

Maggie nodded, swallowing the lump in her throat. "Yes. Luke Axton. He and his daughter Charlotte took care of me while I was recovering."

"You were gone for nearly two weeks," Elaine stated, her face reflecting her concern. "We thought...well, we didn't know what to think."

"I'm sorry," Maggie apologised again, her heart aching at the thought of causing her friends such distress. "I should have sent word."

"Word wouldn't have eased our minds, Maggie," Dorothy reassured her. "Seeing you, knowing you're all right, that's all that matters."

Maggie looked at her friends, their faces reflecting the same relief she felt. "I've missed you both," she said, her voice filled with genuine emotion.

"And we've missed you, Maggie," Elaine replied, giving her a warm smile. "But you're home now. That's all that matters."

As Maggie nodded in agreement, a part of her longed for the comforting presence of Luke and Charlotte, and the home they had provided her, if only for a brief period of time. She was home now, though, with Dorothy and Elaine, and that's where she needed to be. At least, for now.

Elaine's sharp gaze didn't miss the wistful look in Maggie's eyes, nor the soft tone her voice took when she spoke of Luke and Charlotte. After they had eaten their dinner, she sat beside Maggie on the creaky old sofa.

"Maggie," Elaine started, her voice gentle, "you seem... different. Distant, maybe?"

Maggie was silent for a moment, her gaze fixed on the flickering flame of the oil lamp. She bit her lower lip, feeling the warmth rise to her cheeks. "I...I miss them," she confessed quietly.

Elaine gave her a puzzled look. "Miss who?"

"Luke...and Charlotte," Maggie said, her voice barely a whisper. The names hung in the silence of the room, carrying a weight Maggie had been trying to suppress.

Elaine studied Maggie for a moment, her brows furrowed in thought. "You were only with them for a short while, Maggie."

Maggie nodded, her gaze still fixed on the lamp. "I know, but they were...kind to me. Luke saved me, and Charlotte...she was like the little sister I never had."

"And Luke?" Elaine probed, her tone cautious.

Maggie bit her lip harder, her heart pounding in her chest. "Luke..." she sighed, unable to continue. How could she put into words the strange warmth that bloomed in her chest whenever she thought of him? How his kindness had reached her in a way no one else's had?

Elaine didn't say anything, but her soft gaze was enough. Maggie didn't have to voice her feelings; Elaine, always perceptive, already understood. For now, though, the silence was a balm, allowing Maggie to mourn the distance between her and a man she had no right to miss this much.

Chapter 17

A harsh knock resounded through the house as Luke and Charlotte sat down for breakfast, and he winced. Who was it at this hour? With a smile towards Charlotte, he got up to answer.

Only for his expression to fall when he saw none other than Esther, standing on his front step.

Esther's arrival at the house brought an unexpected wave of tension. Luke greeted her politely, his expression guarded as he invited her inside. However, as Esther learned of Maggie's departure, a triumphant smile tugged at the corners of her lips.

"Luke, I'm glad to see that Maggie is no longer here," Esther remarked, her voice laced with a hint of satisfaction. "I knew she didn't belong in our lives. It's for the best."

Luke's brows furrowed, his voice filled with a touch of indignation. "Esther, that's not a kind thing to say. Maggie brought joy and support to our home, and I appreciate the connection we shared."

Esther's smile waned, her eyes narrowing with resentment. "Don't be naive, Luke. She was just a temporary distraction. It's clear that she was interfering with our plans."

Charlotte, who had been listening from a nearby room, couldn't bear to hear Esther speak so callously about Maggie. Her face flushed with indignation as she stepped into the room, her voice filled with defiance.

"Esther, that's not fair!" Charlotte's words rang with a surprising strength. "Maggie was kind and caring. She made us laugh and helped us feel loved. You shouldn't say mean things about her."

Luke's heart swelled with pride at his daughter's defence of Maggie. He stepped forward, his voice calm but firm. "Charlotte is right, Esther. Maggie brought light into our lives, and I won't tolerate cruel words about her. We had something special, and I won't let you dismiss it so callously."

Esther's face contorted with a mix of anger and disbelief. She struggled to find a retort but fell short, realising the depth of her misstep. Silence settled in the room, the weight of their words hanging heavily.

In that moment, Luke understood the truth that had been revealed—a truth about Esther's inability to understand and appreciate the connections that were meaningful to him and Charlotte. The wedge between them had grown wider, and he knew that their paths were diverging.

Luke, despite the heaviness in his heart, made the decision to accept Esther's dinner invitation. He knew it would provide an opportunity to address the growing divide between them and bring closure to their courtship. He hoped that a private setting would allow for an honest conversation.

Esther, her victory seemingly secured, smiled triumphantly as Luke agreed to join her for dinner. She turned to leave, her tone laced with satisfaction. "I'll see you tonight then, Luke. I'm glad we can spend some quality time together."

As Esther departed, her confidence overshadowed by a sense of superiority, Luke couldn't help but feel a mix of relief and trepidation. He knew that the decision he had made was necessary for their own well-being and happiness, but the pain of ending a relationship was never easy.

Turning his attention to Charlotte, he found her on the verge of tears, her eyes still filled with the hurt caused by Esther's words. Luke's heart ached for his daughter, his voice gentle as he approached her.

"Charlotte, my dear, are you all right?" Luke asked, concern etched into his features.

Charlotte's voice quivered as she fought back her tears. "I'm upset, Papa. I don't understand why Esther was so mean to Maggie."

Luke knelt beside Charlotte, his hand reaching out to wipe away a stray tear. "Sometimes, people show their true colours when they feel threatened or when things don't go as they expect. It's important to remember that it's not a reflection of your worth or Maggie's. We will always cherish the kindness and joy she brought into our lives."

Charlotte nodded, her small frame still trembling with a mix of sadness and confusion. "I miss Maggie, Papa. I wish she could be here with us."

Luke embraced his daughter, his voice filled with tenderness. "I miss her too, Charlotte. And I understand how you feel. We will always carry the love and memories of the time we spent together. It's what truly matters."

With a deep sigh, Charlotte composed herself and made her way upstairs to find solace in the comfort of her room. Luke watched her go, his heart heavy with a mix of concern and determination.

***

As the evening approached, Luke readied himself for the dinner with Esther, his mind swirling with a mix of emotions. He knew that ending their courtship was the right decision, but the thought of hurting someone he once cared for still pained him.

Taking a deep breath, Luke straightened his collar, resolving to approach the evening with honesty and compassion. He knew that their paths were diverging, and it was better to acknowledge that truth rather than prolong the inevitable.

Luke entered Charlotte's room with a gentle knock on the door, hoping to convince her to get ready for the evening. However, to his surprise, Charlotte met him with a resolute refusal.

"Charlotte, we can't leave you alone," Luke insisted, his voice filled with concern. "Mrs Yates won't be here tonight, and it's not safe for you to be on your own. Please, reconsider."

Charlotte crossed her arms, her eyes filled with stubborn determination. "I don't want to go, Papa. I don't want to be around Esther anymore. It's not fair how she treated Maggie."

"I understand, Charlotte, but I cannot leave you here alone. I'll give you ten minutes and then we are leaving. Come and get me in my room when you are ready."

Luke's worry deepened as he realised the gravity of the situation. He knew Charlotte was upset and felt betrayed by Esther's actions. He understood her desire to distance herself from the woman who had caused so much hurt.

Ten minutes had passed with no sign of Charlotte. Reluctantly, Luke made his way to the hallway to retrieve Charlotte's coat, determined to convince her to join him. However, as he reached for the coat peg, he noticed it was empty. Confusion clouded his features as he searched the nearby area, but Charlotte's coat was nowhere to be found.

A sense of urgency gripped Luke's heart, and he hurried back to Charlotte's room, his voice tinged with worry. "Charlotte, where is your coat? We need to find it and make sure you're warm enough."

Upon entering her room, Luke found it empty, his concern skyrocketing. Panic gripped him as he searched every nook and cranny, desperately hoping to find a trace of his daughter.

Fear clawed at his chest as he realised the weight of the situation. He couldn't fathom where Charlotte might have gone or how long she had been missing.

With a racing heart, Luke rushed to gather his coat and hat, ready to search the surrounding area for any sign of Charlotte. He knew that time was of the essence, and he couldn't afford to waste a single moment.

As he stepped out into the night, a mixture of fear and determination coursed through his veins. His thoughts raced, his voice a whispered plea in the night. "Please, let Charlotte be safe. Guide me to her."

With that, Luke set off into the darkness, his heart heavy with worry and his mind consumed by the task of finding his beloved daughter. He would leave no stone unturned until he brought her back home, praying that he would find her unharmed and restore the sense of security that had been shattered.

Chapter 18

Maggie was just about to lock the dressmaker's front door when a small figure caught her eye. In the faint glow of the gas lamps, she recognised Charlotte, looking lost and forlorn. Her heart lurched as she hastily reopened the door.

"Charlotte? What on earth are you doing here?" Maggie exclaimed, looking the young girl over. She was still wearing her nightgown, a coat hastily thrown over her shoulders.

Charlotte's eyes brimmed with tears. "I...I ran away," she admitted, her voice shaky. "Papa... he... he wants to stay with Esther!"

Maggie felt a pang in her chest. Esther, the woman who was in love with Luke but didn't want Charlotte, had not been kind to her during her stay. But the thought of Luke marrying her... it felt like a gut punch. "Oh, Charlotte," she murmured, pulling the girl into a hug.

With the shop door shut and locked behind them, Maggie led Charlotte upstairs to her small apartment. She sat Charlotte on her worn couch, fetching her a warm blanket.

Charlotte sniffled, her small hands wringing the fabric of her nightgown. "I don't want her to be my mama," she confessed. "I... I wanted...," but her voice trailed off, her gaze dropping to her lap.

Maggie took a seat beside her, her heart aching for the girl. "You wanted me?" she ventured, her voice barely above a whisper.

Charlotte nodded, the tears rolling down her cheeks. Maggie held her, not knowing what else to do. She felt a strange mixture of pain and disbelief. Luke was moving on, as he should. She had no claim on him.

After a long silence, Maggie gently wiped Charlotte's tears. "We should get you home, love," she said. Charlotte didn't protest, and together they ventured into the cool evening. As they walked in silence, Maggie couldn't help but glance at the house at the end of the street, the house she had come to associate with warmth, care, and a man whose presence was etched into her heart.

Luke's face, illuminated in the soft glow from the house's lantern, was a mix of relief and exhaustion when he opened the door. His eyes instantly found Charlotte, and he rushed to embrace her, relief palpable in his every move.

"Charlotte!" he exclaimed, hugging her tightly, his voice tight. "What were you thinking? Running off like that!"

"I... I was scared," Charlotte confessed, her eyes welling up once again. "I... I didn't want you to marry Esther."

Luke's eyes widened. He glanced at Maggie, a hint of surprise and confusion on his face. "Esther? Where did you get that idea?"

"You said you would go to dinner with her."

Luke sighed, running a hand through his hair. "Charlotte, I wanted to break it off with her. I thought it was better to do so in private."

"Oh," Charlotte murmured, looking a little sheepish.

Luke turned his gaze to Maggie, the gratitude in his eyes sending a warm rush through her. "Maggie... I can't thank you enough."

"It's all right, Luke," she replied, her heart pounding against her chest. "Charlotte's a smart girl. She knew where to go."

Their eyes locked for a moment that seemed to stretch on forever. But then

Charlotte's soft yawn echoed in the silent hallway, breaking the spell.

"I should leave," Maggie said, stepping back. "It's late, and Charlotte must be tired."

Luke nodded, moving to close the door. "Thank you, Maggie," he said one last time, his eyes softening. The door closed with a soft click, leaving Maggie alone in the cool night, the echo of his words warming her heart as she made her way back home.

Chapter 19

The day had started out as typical as any at Mrs Smith's dressmakers. Ladies from all around the city had crowded into the store to request new dresses or to pick up completed ones. Amid the bustling shop, Esther stormed in, her face contorted into a scowl.

"Maggie!" she called out, her voice louder than necessary. The customers instantly fell silent, and all eyes turned to the unfolding drama. Maggie looked up from the dress she was pinning, surprise evident on her face.

"Esther?" she said, a tinge of concern evident in her voice. "What's wrong?"

"What's wrong?" Esther spat, "You're what's wrong, Maggie. You and your little charade."

Maggie blinked in surprise. "What are you talking about, Esther?"

"Don't act all innocent," Esther pointed a trembling finger at her. "I know you're the reason why Luke doesn't want to be with me."

Mrs Smith had stopped her work and was eyeing the altercation nervously, "Ladies, this is no place to—"

"Oh, shut up, Mrs Smith!" Esther snapped, silencing the older woman. The entire shop was holding its breath, waiting for the next salvo in the unfolding spectacle.

Maggie stared at Esther for a moment before sighing. "Esther, I've never done anything to come between you and Luke. You're mistaken."

"Mistaken?" Esther shrieked, causing more than a few customers to jump. "Don't think I'm a fool, Maggie. I've seen the way you look at him, and the way he looks at you!"

Despite the commotion, Maggie maintained her composure. "Esther, you're upset. This isn't the place to discuss this."

Esther's face reddened, and for a moment, Maggie thought she might physically attack her. But instead, Esther turned on her heel, her voice raised in a huff. "You'll regret this, Maggie!"

And with that, she stormed out of the dressmaker's shop, leaving behind a stunned silence. The shock of the incident hung heavy in the air. Maggie looked around at the shocked faces of the women in the shop, then at Mrs Smith.

"Maggie," Mrs Smith began, "what just transpired out there was completely unacceptable. The store is a place of business, not a stage for public brawls."

Maggie bit her lip, glancing down at the ground. "I know, Mrs Smith," she said quietly. "I'm sorry."

"Sorry isn't enough, Maggie. This store's reputation could be damaged because of your personal affairs. This behaviour can't be tolerated."

"I understand, ma'am," Maggie said, "It won't happen again."

But Mrs Smith wasn't finished. "Maggie, I've always held you in high regard. You're hardworking, talented and the customers like you. After today's incident... I'm afraid I can't have you in the shop anymore."

Maggie felt her heart drop. "What? Mrs Smith, I didn't—"

The older woman held up a hand to silence her. "I've made my decision, Maggie. I'm letting you go. I can't risk another scene like this. It's bad for business."

"But Mrs Smith, it wasn't my fault," Maggie protested, her voice shaking slightly. "Esther came in here and—"

"I understand that, dear," Mrs Smith interrupted, her voice gentler now, but firm.

"But the fact remains that your presence provoked that confrontation. It's unfortunate, but it's for the best."

Maggie stared at her former employer, shock leaving her speechless. She had not anticipated the day's turn of events. Fired? But she needed this job; it was her livelihood, her passion.

"But where will I—"

"I'm sorry, Maggie," Mrs Smith cut her off, her face remaining impassive. "This is non-negotiable."

With that, she turned away, leaving Maggie alone with the echo of her words. A profound silence hung in the small room, wrapping Maggie in its chilling grip. She was at a loss. She had just lost her job, been humiliated publicly, and been dragged into a conflict she wanted no part in. The reality of her situation was slowly sinking in, filling her with a sense of dread. She was suddenly on her own, her path uncertain, her future unclear.

As Maggie made the trek back to their tenement, each step felt heavier than the last. Her mind was filled with thoughts of uncertainty and anxiety. She barely noticed the bustling city around her, her focus consumed by her own turmoil. She wanted to break down and cry, to shout at the injustice of it all. But she knew that wouldn't solve anything.

Upon reaching their tenement, Maggie found Elaine alone, busily mending a tear in an old dress. Elaine looked up at Maggie's entrance and immediately sensed that something was wrong. Maggie's face was pale, her eyes weary and filled with an indefinable sadness. "Maggie, what happened?" Elaine asked, setting aside her work.

Maggie swallowed, fighting back the tears threatening to spill over. "I... I lost my job."

Elaine blinked in surprise, then stood, rushing over to her friend. "What? How did that happen?"

Maggie sank onto a nearby chair, the weight of her troubles finally catching up to her. She relayed the day's events to Elaine, who listened attentively, her expression growing more and more concerned.

"Oh, Maggie," Elaine breathed out when Maggie finished her tale. "I'm so sorry."

Maggie shrugged, attempting a weak smile that didn't quite reach her eyes. "It's not your fault, Elaine."

"I know, but I..." Elaine paused, choosing her words carefully. "I worry about you. About all of us."

"I know," Maggie said quietly. "I worry too. Without my pay, we'll struggle to make the rent."

Elaine nodded, her brow furrowing in thought. "We'll figure something out, Maggie. We always do."

The sentiment was nice, but both of them knew that their situation was dire. The prospect of losing their home, of being forced out onto the streets, was a harsh reality they had to consider. Elaine reached out, squeezing Maggie's hand in a comforting gesture.

For a moment, they sat in silence, their minds consumed by their predicament. The tenement around them felt unusually quiet, as if the walls themselves were holding their breath, waiting to see what would happen next. Maggie felt a wave of despair wash over her. But she also felt a flicker of determination ignite within her. She was not going to let this setback defeat her. She would fight, for Elaine, for Dorothy, and most importantly, for herself.

Elaine began to brainstorm, her eyes bright with determination. "There's the bakery down the street," she suggested, "They could use some help."

Maggie shook her head, a wan smile touching her lips. "You know I can't bake, Elaine. I'd probably burn the place down."

The two women shared a tired laugh. Elaine was silent for a moment before proposing another idea, "What about Mrs Miller? She could use a hand with her children."

Again, Maggie shook her head. "I appreciate your efforts, Elaine, but I can't accept that kind of job. I'm not cut out for childcare."

Elaine's suggestions continued, each one met with a polite, albeit weary, rejection from Maggie. The options were limited and none seemed promising. They were grasping at straws, hoping against hope for a solution that would keep them from the looming threat of homelessness.

Despite Elaine's attempts to lift her spirits, Maggie felt the burden of their predicament settle heavily on her shoulders. Guilt gnawed at her. She knew it wasn't entirely her fault, but she couldn't help blaming herself. She was the one who had lost her job. She was the one who had allowed Esther's words to affect her. And now, she was the one who had put them all at risk.

The room was silent again, the brainstorming session having come to a standstill. Maggie stared blankly at the floor, her mind a whirl of thoughts and worries. Elaine, sensing her friend's distress, reached out and gently took Maggie's hand.

"Maggie," she began, her voice gentle, "You can't blame yourself for what happened. You did nothing wrong."

"But I..."

"No," Elaine interrupted, squeezing Maggie's hand for emphasis, "Esther is to blame for this, not you. And we will get through it, just like we always do."

Maggie wanted to believe Elaine, wanted to let go of the guilt that was eating away at her. But it wasn't that simple. The sense of responsibility was too great, the consequences of her job loss too severe. Even as Elaine spoke words of comfort and reassurance, Maggie couldn't help but feel the weight of their situation pressing down on her.

They were in a precarious position, teetering on the edge of a steep cliff. One wrong step, one more piece of bad news, and they could all tumble down into an abyss of poverty and uncertainty. And despite Elaine's words, Maggie couldn't shake the feeling that she was the one who had brought them to the brink.

Chapter 20

Luke had been nursing a cup of tea in the sitting room when Mrs Yates came bustling in, a basket of freshly ironed linens in her hands. Her face was creased with concern, and she set the basket down on a nearby chair before taking a seat opposite him.

"Mr Axton," she began, clasping her hands in her lap. "I visited the dressmaker's today to fetch a parcel. I was hoping to catch a glimpse of Miss Barlow, but she wasn't there."

Luke set his teacup down, his eyebrows furrowing in surprise. "She wasn't? That's odd. Did Mrs Smith say where she was?"

Mrs Yates shook her head, her expression troubled. "No, Mr Axton. Mrs Smith simply said that Maggie no longer works there. She gave no indication of where she might have gone."

A knot of worry formed in Luke's stomach, a stark contrast to the comforting warmth of the tea he had been sipping. The last time he had seen Maggie, she had seemed...not quite herself. Troubled. And now, she was gone from her job with no explanation.

"I see," he said, trying to keep the concern out of his voice. "Perhaps she found work elsewhere."

Mrs Yates merely shrugged, her face reflecting his own worries. "Perhaps, Mr

Axton. But I fear that something may be wrong."

The thought was like a cold splash of water. He had been nursing a fondness for Maggie, one that had grown stronger each day since he saved her from that drunken sailor. He had found himself thinking of her often, her spirit and determination, her dedication to her family. The thought that she might be in trouble was a bitter pill to swallow.

"I don't suppose you have any idea where she might live, Mrs Yates?" Luke asked, already knowing the answer.

Mrs Yates shook her head again, her lips pressed into a thin line. "I'm afraid not, sir."

The room fell silent, the ticking of the grandfather clock in the corner echoing loudly in his ears. His thoughts were consumed by Maggie, her disappearance from her job, and the lingering worry that something was amiss. He had no way to contact her, no way to ensure she was safe. It was a helpless feeling, one that left a bitter taste in his mouth as he finished his now lukewarm tea.

***

The bustle of the dressmaker's was a stark contrast to the quiet turmoil that had taken over Luke's mind. He entered the shop, his eyes scanning the room for any sign of Maggie. Mrs Smith was at the counter, dealing with a customer, her stern face reminding him of why he was there.

Seeing no sign of Maggie, Luke walked up to a young seamstress who was busy pinning a dress on a mannequin. She looked up in surprise as he approached, her eyes wide.

"Excuse me, miss," he said, trying to keep his voice steady. "I'm looking for Maggie Barlow. She used to work here."

The seamstress blushed, looking uncomfortable. "I-I'm sorry, sir. Maggie... Maggie doesn't work here anymore."

Luke's heart sank at the confirmation. "Yes, we heard. But do you know why she left? Was there a problem?"

The seamstress hesitated, glancing nervously over at Mrs Smith who was now free of her customer. But she seemed to make up her mind, turning back to Luke with a determined look.

"She didn't leave, sir," she whispered, leaning closer so that Mrs Smith wouldn't hear. "She was fired. There was an argument... with a customer."

An argument? Luke could hardly imagine Maggie, who was so gentle and polite, getting into an argument. His mind immediately went to one person. Esther. His disappointment was profound.

"Do you know who this customer was?" he asked, trying to keep his voice neutral.

The seamstress shook her head. "No, sir. But she was a tall lady, well-dressed, with a high voice. Mrs Smith was really upset about the whole thing."

The description fit Esther perfectly. Luke felt a surge of disappointment. He couldn't believe she would cause such a scene, let alone get Maggie fired. But then again, he had noticed Esther's jealousy of Maggie. He just didn't think she would go this far.

"Thank you, miss," Luke said, giving the seamstress a reassuring smile. "You've been very helpful."

He briskly walked over to Mrs Smith. "I have an urgent matter, Ma'am. It's concerning Miss Barlow. Can you please provide her address to me?"

Mrs Smith looked at him. She wanted to refuse but she knew that Mr Darby was grooming him to take over the warehouse when he retired. "Let me find her application; that should have her address on. Give me a moment."

Minutes later, Mrs Smith returned. Luke said nothing as he angrily grabbed the paper from her hand.

As he left the shop, Luke was filled with a new determination. He would find Maggie and make things right. Now that he knew where she lived, he would visit her, apologise for Esther's behaviour, and maybe... just maybe... he could convince her to come back.

But for now, he had to break the news to Charlotte and Mrs Yates who waited for him outside. As they walked down the street, he sighed, ready to face whatever came next. He just hoped that Maggie was okay.

The tenement building where Maggie lived was a far cry from the comfortable surroundings of Luke's own home. As he, Charlotte, and Mrs Yates approached the structure, he was taken aback by the state of disrepair it was in. The exterior of the building was crumbling, the bricks and plaster covered in a layer of soot and grime from years of neglect.

Children were playing in the dirt-laden courtyard, their clothes ragged and faces streaked with dirt. They seemed blissfully unaware of their surroundings, their laughter echoing off the grimy walls. Their joy did little to lessen the sombre atmosphere that pervaded the area.

Luke pushed against the rusted metal gate leading into the building. It creaked in protest, the years of disuse and neglect evident in the flaking rust and worn hinges. Once inside, he found the interior of the building to be just as bleak.

The hallway was dimly lit, the bare wooden floorboards creaking underfoot. The air was heavy with a musty smell, the scent of old damp wood mingling with the faint odour of cooking from the various apartments.

His heart ached at the thought of Maggie living in those conditions. He had always known that she lived modestly, but he had no idea that her circumstances were this bleak. As they ascended the narrow staircase to the floor where Maggie's apartment was, his concern for her grew.

He glanced at Charlotte, who was looking around with wide eyes. He could tell that she too was affected by what she was seeing. It was a stark reminder of how different their lives were from Maggie's.

Reaching Maggie's door, Luke knocked softly, apprehensive about what they might find inside. The sound seemed to echo in the quiet hallway, the silence only reinforcing his worry.

His mind raced with thoughts of Maggie, her bright smile and warm eyes. How had she managed to retain such a cheerful spirit living in such conditions? The thought only increased his admiration for her and solidified his resolve to help her.

When the door finally opened, it revealed a weary yet resilient Maggie. A pang of relief washed over Luke. He immediately took in her appearance - her rosy cheeks a bit too pale, her usual sparkle a bit dimmed. But she was here, and she was safe.

She looked startled at their sudden visit, taking a step back as she registered their presence. Luke quickly reassured her, explaining their worry when they didn't find her at the dressmaker's shop.

It took a bit of convincing, but Maggie eventually allowed them into her humble abode. The inside was in stark contrast to the outside of the building. It was clear she took care of her home, even if it was simple and worn. The rooms were clean, with a comforting warmth that spoke volumes about the woman who lived there.

"Luke... Why are you here?" Maggie asked, her gaze focused on him. The question was simple, direct, but underlined by an undercurrent of uncertainty.

Before Luke could answer, Charlotte interjected. "We were worried about you, Maggie," she said, her innocent candour cutting through the tension in the room. "You weren't at the dressmaker's, and we didn't know where you were."

There was a moment of silence as Maggie processed Charlotte's words. Then, she let out a sigh, a mix of exhaustion and relief. She looked at Luke, her eyes revealing a hint of the turmoil she must be going through.

Chapter 21

Luke's heart beat rapidly in his chest as he watched Maggie, her eyes wide and unguarded in her surprise at their unexpected visit.

"Maggie," Luke began, his voice strained with worry and relief. "We...we were worried when you weren't at the dressmaker's."

She chewed her bottom lip, a sure sign of her discomfort. "You shouldn't be here, Luke," she said, her words spoken softly, but with a firmness that underscored her sentiment.

"Why not?" It was Charlotte who asked, her childish innocence cutting through the tension. She tried to peek around Maggie, her curiosity piqued.

"Charlotte..." Luke murmured a warning, but the little girl paid him no mind.

Maggie sighed, her shoulders slumping slightly. She gave Luke a look - a mix of resentment and embarrassment. "You've seen where I work, Luke, and now you want to see where I live? I've got no grand home to show off."

Luke felt a pang of regret at her words. "That's not why we're here, Maggie," he said, holding her gaze earnestly. "You weren't at work, and we were worried something might've happened to you."

"Really?" she asked, her scepticism thinly veiled.

Luke nodded, his concern for her evident in his gaze. "Yes."

Luke offered her a small, grateful smile as he walked into her modest home, feeling an odd mix of relief and concern. Even though they were here under less than ideal circumstances, he was glad to know she was safe. That was what mattered the most to him.

As they stepped inside Maggie's home, Luke was aware of a knot of emotions tightening in his chest. The room, modest but immaculately kept, echoed Maggie's resilience and spirit. He glanced at Mrs Yates and Charlotte, their concerned faces mirroring his own apprehension.

"Maggie, I…" Luke began, only to falter as he struggled to find the right words. He'd always been a man of actions, not words, and now, faced with the woman he had grown to care for, he felt inadequately prepared to express his feelings.

"I..." he tried again, his gaze returning to Maggie, whose expression was unreadable. "I... I broke things off with Esther," he confessed. There was a collective gasp, a slight widening of eyes, but he couldn't tell who had reacted first. "And it's because... because I realised my feelings... my feelings for you, Maggie."

Maggie blinked at him, clearly caught off-guard. "Luke," she started, her voice barely audible. He raised his hand slightly, asking silently for her to let him finish.

"I love you, Maggie," he declared, his voice resolute. The moment the words left his lips, he felt a profound sense of relief wash over him. "I've tried to hide it, to deny it, but I can't anymore. I... I love you."

Silence stretched out, almost tangible in its intensity. Mrs Yates and Charlotte looked at him, then at Maggie, their faces a canvas of surprise and apprehension. Luke felt his heart hammering in his chest as he waited for Maggie to respond.

Luke moved forward, gently taking Maggie's hands in his. "Maggie," he murmured, his voice just above a whisper. "I have no ring to give you, and I know this is not how these things are usually done, but... will you marry me?"

The room was deathly quiet. The world seemed to hold its breath. His declaration hung in the air, heavy with anticipation. His heart pounded in his chest, and he realised that his future was no longer in his hands. It was in hers.

Chapter 22

Maggie felt her world spin as Luke's words echoed through her mind. A flood of emotions washed over her, rendering her momentarily speechless. His words hung heavy in the air between them, an open confession and an invitation, all at once.

"Yes," she whispered, her voice trembling with the weight of her emotions. Then, louder, "Yes, Luke. I'll marry you."

She felt the words pour from her heart, filling the room with a warmth that seemed to radiate from her very soul. There was an audible sigh of relief from Luke, and the tension seemed to evaporate from his body.

"I love you too, Luke," she confessed, her eyes glistening with unshed tears. "I've been in love with you, and I've been hiding it, thinking you'd never feel the same way."

Her gaze shifted to Charlotte, the innocent child whose presence had grown to mean so much to her. "And you, Charlotte. I love you too. I'd be honoured to be a part of your life."

Charlotte's eyes widened in surprise, before her face split into a wide grin. "Really, Maggie?" she squealed, her joy infectious. "You want to be my mother?"

Maggie reached out, gently brushing a lock of hair from the young girl's face. "More than anything, Charlotte. More than anything," she affirmed, her heart swelling with affection for the little girl who was already so dear to her.

She could see the relief and joy in Luke's eyes, mirroring her own feelings. This was right. This was what she wanted. A family. A home. Love.

In the quiet of her modest room, surrounded by the man and the child she loved, Maggie felt a deep sense of belonging. A sense of peace that she hadn't felt in a long time.

Maggie stared at Luke in shock, her heart pounding at the sudden proposal. His words were a promise of a life she'd never dared to imagine. A life of security, love, and, most importantly, family. Charlotte's excited chattering was a lovely background to the intense gaze that Luke was directing at her.

The connection between them was electrifying. She never thought she could feel this way about someone. This intensity, this warmth, this indescribable sense of belonging. Her breath hitched as Luke's fingers gently brushed her cheek, and she closed her eyes, basking in his touch.

Then came the soft pressure of his lips on hers. A rush of emotions overwhelmed her, a silent confession of her feelings that words couldn't capture. It was sweet, tender and completely disarming. Her first kiss.

When she opened her eyes, she could see her reflection in Luke's gaze – a woman loved, cherished. She was on the verge of tears, a mix of joy, gratitude, and disbelief.

And then Luke presented her with another surprise. A key to a dressmaker's shop. Her own shop. The shock was potent, her mind struggling to grasp the enormity of his gift.

"Luke, that's too much," she protested, but he silenced her with a look.

"No, Maggie, it's not. You deserve it," he insisted, his gaze turning soft as he glanced at Charlotte. "It's for our future. For our family."

His words filled her with a warmth that spread from the top of her head to the soles of her feet. Their future. Their family. It felt right, it felt good.

Her mind started racing with the possibilities. With her own shop, she could provide opportunities for girls like her, underprivileged and in need. She could help them find their way out of poverty, just like she had. It would be her way of giving back, of making a difference.

Wiping the tears that threatened to spill from her eyes, she looked at Luke. His eyes were full of hope, love, and a hint of apprehension, probably wondering if he had overstepped boundaries.

"Yes, Luke," she finally whispered, offering him a watery smile, "I love the idea of having our own shop. We can make it a haven for girls like me. We can help them."

His relieved smile was all the response she needed. With those words, she felt like she had truly found her place in the world. With Luke and Charlotte. With her future family. She was home.

Epilogue

One year later

Maggie took a deep breath, staring at her reflection in the dusty mirror that hung in the tiny room she had prepared herself in. Today was her wedding day. A gentle knock at the door drew her away from her thoughts, and she turned around to see Elaine and Dorothy standing there, their eyes wide and teary.

"Are you ready, Maggie?" Elaine asked softly, her voice thick with emotion. Maggie simply nodded, her hands clasping and unclasping in a show of her nervous excitement.

"I'm ready," Maggie assured them, her voice stronger than she felt.

She slipped her arms into theirs, feeling a rush of gratitude towards the women who had become her family. It wasn't traditional for brides to be escorted down the aisle by women, but she had no man in her life to do the honour, and she wouldn't have it any other way.

As they started walking down the aisle, her heart pounded in her chest. Luke was waiting for her at the end of the aisle, his face a mask of emotion that brought tears to her eyes. He was dressed in a handsome, simple suit that made his eyes even more striking than usual.

Victorian tradition dictated that the bride should wear white, a symbol of her purity. And so, she did. But she didn't do it for tradition. She did it for Luke. She did it for herself. She wore a dress of the softest white lace, hand-sewn by the girls she had started to employ at the dressmaker's shop. Every stitch was a symbol of their gratitude and love, and she was proud to be wearing it.

As she reached the altar, she looked around the small chapel. It was simple, adorned only with fresh flowers that the girls had picked from the nearby fields. But it was perfect. It was them. It was their love, simple and beautiful.

Her gaze landed on the empty pew that was meant to be for her family. She couldn't help the pang of sadness that filled her. She wished her brothers could be here, to see how

far she had come. But she knew they were
with her, in spirit.

Turning her attention back to Luke, she
took his hands in hers, her eyes welling up
with tears. She could see the love in his eyes,
feel the warmth of his hands. This was the
man she was going to spend the rest of her life
with. This was the man she loved.

"I do," she whispered, her voice
echoing in the chapel. She watched as Luke's
lips echoed her words, his hands squeezing
hers in reassurance.

As the vicar announced them husband
and wife, she leaned into Luke, letting him
take her into his arms. His lips were warm and
tender on hers, and she felt her heart swell
with happiness.

She was married. She was Maggie Axton, the wife of Luke Axton, the mother of Charlotte Axton. She had a family, a life she loved.

And as she looked around, seeing the smiling faces of the people she loved, she knew she had found her happiness.

***

So much had happened in the past year.

Mr. Darby had passed six months before Maggie and Luke were married, and he had left the warehouse, a pair of sailing ships, and his export business to Luke. Luke had prospered as a merchant and loved working in the export business. Maggie found it hard to believe the life that she was now living. She feared it was only a dream and that she would wake up one day back at the tenement building.

Maggie sat at the breakfast table, quietly enjoying the early morning peace of her new home. Luke was already up, reading the newspaper in his usual place across from her. A soft smile graced her lips as she watched him, the silent contentment of their domesticity warming her heart.

"Luke," she said, breaking the comfortable silence. She wasn't sure what prompted her to voice her thoughts out loud, but the words were out before she could think twice. "I've been thinking about William and Thomas..."

Luke lowered his newspaper, his gaze meeting hers across the table. "What about them?" he asked, his voice steady and calm.

Before she could respond, he interrupted her. "Maggie," he said, his voice serious, "I need to tell you something. I... I hired a private investigator."

Her breath hitched, the implications of his words dawning on her. "You found them?" she whispered, her voice barely audible over the clinking of their cutlery on the plates.

He nodded, his face solemn. "Yes, I did," he said. "I found them, and I offered them jobs at my warehouse and lodgings until they are of age. They accepted."

Her heart pounded in her chest. She was going to see her brothers again, after so long apart. She could hardly believe it, her mind struggling to catch up with the whirlwind of emotions that flooded her.

Tears welled in her eyes, overwhelming gratitude flooding her as she looked at her husband. She couldn't form the words, her heart too full, but she didn't need to. Luke reached across the table, taking her hand in his, and gave it a reassuring squeeze.

"I thought we could go see them today, if you feel up to it," he suggested, his voice gentle. "I think they would be overjoyed to see their sister."

Maggie nodded, wiping her tears away with her free hand. "Yes," she managed to say, her voice choked with emotion. "Yes, I'd like that very much."

As they finished their breakfast, Maggie couldn't help but marvel at the wonderful turn her life had taken. She had a loving husband, a new daughter, and now, she was going to be reunited with her brothers.

Looking across the table at Luke, her heart overflowed with love. This man, who had come into her life and turned it around, had not only given her a new life, but also given her back her family. She was grateful, more than she could ever express, and she knew she would spend the rest of her life showing him just how much she loved him.

***

The scent of blooming flowers filled the air as they approached the park. Sunlight was fading into dusk, washing the sky in hues of orange and red. The anticipation was a palpable weight in Maggie's chest, making her heart flutter like a trapped bird. She held onto

Luke's hand, his steady grip providing a grounding comfort.

And there they were, her brothers, waiting by the park's central fountain. The sight of them made her heart clench, a flood of memories rushing back. She barely recognised them; they had grown taller, their faces matured, the boyish charm replaced by an adult-like demeanour.

"William! Thomas!" She couldn't hold back the excited cry that escaped her lips, her eyes welling up with tears. She felt Luke squeeze her hand encouragingly.

They turned at the sound of her voice, their eyes wide and incredulous. For a moment, they just stood there, frozen, before they rushed towards her. Maggie's heart pounded as she watched them close the distance, their faces a mirror of her own joy.

As they reached her, their arms enveloped her in a tight, bone-crushing hug. She felt tears slip down her cheeks, a burst of laughter escaping her lips. The world around her seemed to dissolve into nothingness, leaving only the three of them, united after years of separation.

"Oh, Maggie!" William exclaimed, his voice thick with emotion. "We didn't believe it when Mr Axton's investigator found us. We thought it was a dream."

"I've missed you so much," she confessed, holding them tighter. Their familiar scents, mixed with the harsh reality of their past, brought back a flood of memories. She laughed and cried at the same time, overwhelmed with happiness.

As the tears subsided, they pulled away slightly, looking at each other with wide grins. Their hands were still holding her tightly as if afraid she would disappear. She marvelled at the familiar yet grown-up faces in front of her.

She introduced them to Luke and Charlotte, her new family. The brothers were respectful and gracious, extending their gratitude to Luke for everything he had done. In the shared laughter and happiness, her old and new families were merging into one.

As the sun sank below the horizon and the stars began to twinkle, they sat down on the park's bench, talking, laughing, sharing their lives over the years. Maggie watched the play of emotions on her brothers' faces as they listened to her story. The painful void that had been in her heart for so long was finally beginning to heal. The reunion was more than she could have ever imagined.

"I love you both so much," she said, her voice shaky. Their responding smiles were all the confirmation she needed. As she bid them goodbye, promising to visit soon, she felt a sense of wholeness she hadn't experienced in years.

As they walked back, Luke's arm around her, she whispered a heartfelt thank you, her voice choking up. "This... this means the world to me."

His response was simple, filled with love and understanding, "Anything for you, love."

That night, as she fell asleep in Luke's arms, her heart was full. For the first time in a long time, Maggie felt like she was truly home.

Printed in Great Britain
by Amazon